INTERVIEW
WITH THE
DEVIL

Published in the United States of America.

ISBN: 978-0-692-87225-3

1. Fiction/Fantasy/Dark Fantasy
2. Fiction/Horror

INTERVIEW
WITH THE
DEVIL

PART 1

SKYLERR DARREN

1

. . . .

There, this thing sat at the end of its chair in a seemingly peaceful yet awkwardly disturbing silence. The chair creaked with each movement this being made, leading me to believe this chair must have been worn out due to the raggedy appearance of it. Its original color looked to be as if it were brown, but due to years of abuse, the color had settled to a rusty beige. The chair's poor appearance fit perfectly with the rest of the room's depressed state. The walls had deep cracks driven into the centers, which were uncleverly disguised with patches of duct tape.

The room smelled awful and offensive to the nose, like I had stepped foot into a mummy's tomb. The being's bed lay flat on the cold, hard floor, with a bed sheet no thinner than a piece of white paper and a small dusty pillow covered in brown dirt spots. The bed looked untouched and neat, which led me to wonder if the thing even slept in it or if it even slept at all.

Of all the room's diseased misfortunes, it could never be comparable to what dwelled in its four walls. A monster.

An absolute product of Satan himself. I often wonder to myself if it would even be considered an insult to Satan to place him in the same category of this beast. What in God's name did I get myself into? I had second thoughts about what my insensible mind had been directing me to do the further I stepped into that room, but for some reason, I couldn't cease the seduction. Eccentrically, it's as if the bloodcurdling and sinister aspects of the macabre room had pinned down and constrained the residue of my intuition, similar to a fragile, languid, and horrifically cut-open individual being vigorously bound and painfully violated; and although the being in it would cause the ugliest of all abominations to turn away, I couldn't bring myself to turn around and walk out. I guess I could say that the nightmarish atmosphere attracted me. As if it had been interesting that a so-called human being could actually even live this way. That a human being could do such things to get locked away in seclusion like an accursed, cannibalistic miscreation, exactly what this grotesque aberration had been. A breathing deformity. I couldn't even envision something this hideous coming out of a human woman.

What was this thing, and what was it about? My soul filled itself with determination and confidence to find that one true answer, and I could tell so when my body made able to find a seat in one of the chairs and gave my tongue the ability to say hello. I spoke to the being sitting in the chair. He acted as if he didn't even hear my greeting, and by the disgusting looks of his bruised, distorted ears, it arose to me that he may not even able to properly hear. I sat in my seat nervously, sweat dripping from my forehead and down to my upper lip and formulating between the cracks of my fingers. My leg began to frantically tremble, like it always does when I become restlessly disturbed.

I had been in no condition to induce a conversation with this person, and I appreciated the fact that he too appeared to be in no urgency. I waited patiently for a response that seemed like I wouldn't be receiving any time soon. This gave me a few minutes to look around the room, studying the imperfections of the building structure and further feeding my curiosity.

How could someone wake up and go to sleep viewing these nauseating walls every single day of their life and be perfectly fine? I thought to myself. The molded walls aroused sickness in me just looking at them, and I had only been in that room for a little over five minutes. I tried to avoid eye contact with this thing as much as possible. Truthfully, his presence intimidated me. The experience felt similar to feeding a caged lion with meat behind metal bars; although you're guarded, it's still frightening.

I had no idea what his disarranged mind would make him capable of doing, and I didn't want to find out. I had heard that at the age of fourteen years old, he had pulled a kid's eyes out of the socket with a lobster fork before stabbing him to death with the serrated implement, proceeding on violently raping the child's bleeding, mutilated eye socket; so not looking at him may have been the best thing that I could have done.

His whole body manner seemed off. He rocked back and forth in his chair, nodding his head as if a tune had been being injected into his damaged, misshapened ears. He showed no real human emotion whatsoever. If I could say anything, I'd say that that was the best damn poker face that anyone has ever pulled off. He had his hands crossed in his lap, allowing me to take notice of his hands bound in chains for my protection. He remained content. Relaxed. He hummed that tune as if the bedraggled infirmary that he resided in didn't exist, and he had been sitting outside on a ligneous porch, enjoying the gust and drinking a crisp refreshing beverage. The fact that he came off as so calm in such a state that he had to be restrained in chains to prevent himself from harming others proved that he might not be so right in the head.

He looked at the walls as if it had been his first time being in the institution as well, or if he had been mentally constructing a masterpiece. I contemplated on whether or not I should address him again. I couldn't take the silence any longer. It began to eat me up inside. I took a small gulp and greeted the man once more. His pupils froze for an abrupt second and slowly found their way facing me. His eyes reminded me of the sight of an unattended, gruesomely infected wound, yellow and dripping in water-like pus, and the preternatural colorant of his grody optics made him look as if he had been suffering from a terminal disease. His pupils looked as cadaverous as him, bloodless and clear in pigment, although the way he stared made them sometimes appear as atramentous as night. He had dark swollen bags depressingly glued underneath his eyes, which made his physical appearance even more unappealing.

There sat a frail, abnormally pallid African-American man. His weight appeared rather questionable; he looked as if he hadn't eaten in months, judging by the fact that his integral skeleton had been visible through his diminished skin, revealing his seemingly shattered, poorly repaired ribcage. His bones gnarled and wrenched similar to a twisted hanger, making it appear as though I had been sitting in front of an animated, deformed X-ray. I spied the deteriorated bones poking from out of the disunited scraps of loose, seemingly dead skin scattered across his fingers as he positioned them in his friable lap. His eyebrows looked like the end of a well overused broom, bushy and unkempt, and they hovered over his eyes. Lusterless, kinky black hair laid on the top of his knurled head in a somnolent manner, dusty and shoulder length, bearing a resemblance to braided rope, tangled and matted and overall filthy. His clothes matched the same color as the walls and furniture of his room, beige and dull. He wore a long-sleeved shirt, long sweatpants, and short gray socks with a black strip across the middle.

He stared at me with no facial expression. He just sat there, staring. He didn't move a muscle. He didn't even blink; he just stared. His eyes gave off the impression that he did not want to be bothered. I had threatened him by invading his territory and fixing my mouth to say hello, and I could see it by the way he looked at me. I had been trying to engage in a conversation with a mannequin. What a lifeless figure. After staring at me for what seemed to be an eternity, he cracked his neck. The crack sounded as if he had broken a bone.

I looked at him, agitated, preparing myself for what he'll do next. He cracked his fingers and cleared his throat, and finally he blinked his deserted eyes. He stretched his mouth and made a gesture, leading me to believe that he would begin to speak, and to my prediction, he did.

"Who are you, and why do you come?"

His voice startled me. He spoke with such malevolence. I could almost feel the fires of hell as he opened his mouth. God, were his teeth foul. This living horror didn't contain teeth, but fangs, and they hung from the inside of his decayed mouth like a bat in a cave. Murky, green bacteria coated the outer layers of his teeth, allowing them to appear similar to the rotted skin of the deceased, some of them chipped like one's broken fingernail. The majority of them had already decomposed and fallen out. His breath smelled like roadkill and seemed to make the room more gloomier than it had already been.

I hesitated to give him a response. "I'm Victor Florence, Vick for short," I managed to mumble. "Staff granted me permission to speak with you to get a clearer understanding of why you're in here."

He nodded his head and stared at me with no motion in his eyes. "Get a clearer understanding of why I'm in here?" he asked without procrastination. He began chuckling as if I had said something slightly humorous while maintaining the motionless look on his face. "So you're one of those people who gets a kick out of interviewing murderers and psychopaths so you can exploit them to the media for your own profit, now am I right?"

He puzzled me. "Not at all, sir. I am not here to exploit you. This is actually an assignment given to me by my psychology professor," I said to him, trying to make light of my intention.

He nodded his head. "I'm having a hard time believing that, son, because I've been living in this pile of shit for the last twenty-nine years, since I was seventeen years old, and I haven't been allowed not one visitor. No one is allowed to come in contact with me. I am too dangerous for the general population. I can't even use plastic silverware, they're afraid I might cut someone's neck open with a plastic knife, like that's even probable. Though wouldn't it be a delight if it were. I'd finally receive a decent goddamn meal for once. I'd love to gouge open the neck of the little bitch who threw me in here and patch up the scraped laceration with her dying entrails. So don't lie to me. I don't like being lied to, and I'm not one to be lied to. The last person who lied to me found pieces of their severed tongue in a mouse trap."

The room stood silent. I couldn't believe what he just said. My body sat still, like I was the one in those chains. My heart beat increased, pumping rapidly and nearly bursting from out of my chest. I sat back in my seat, thinking about what I should say that wouldn't anger him. And the worst part about all of this could've been the fact that he didn't even seem angry. This man had just threatened me, but he showed no sign of wrath at all. Those pale walls had more emotion than he did. I tried to reconcile with him.

"With all due respect, I mean no harm. I just thought it would be interesting to speak one on one with a patient from Chy-Merikal Creek Psychiatric Hospital, the top asylum in the state of El Paso, Texas. I'm studying to be a psychologist, and as an assignment, my professor thought it would be favorable to come here and speak to a patient in order to receive experience for something I'll be doing for a living."

Trying to explain to this man that I had no intention of exploiting him proved to be anything but simple. He sat up and coughed, stretching his arms and causing his chains to ghoulishly rattle, sounding like one having their neck stabbed open and their vocal cords brutally removed.

"Understand, bastard, I don't know who you think you are, some sort of community college know-it-all who thinks they're going to get something out of me. You're mistaken if you think you will. There is nothing interesting about me, and you're more lost than I am if you think you're going to help me. You can't help me. I am already gone." His eyes lit up with excitement but still remained physically dead. "You think talking to me is going to be interesting because I'm in a damn nut house? I'm 100 percent positive you communicate with over five people a day that need to be in these four walls, but you find no use of them. How am I any different? I just got caught."

He refrained from talking and resorted back to staring at me. I had never voluntarily peered into the eyes of a corpse. He knew the way he stared at me made me uneasy, yet he continued to do it. And it was something about him that told me I just may receive a benefit. But how did I end up here? I thought I wanted to hear this man's story. Truth is, once it started, I wanted it to end. Who knew that one person could affect someone both mentally and physically, especially a person of this monster's caliber. It didn't have to end up like this. It sure didn't start like this, I'll assure you of that.

2

. . . .

My full name is Victor David Florence, Vick for short, as I had mentioned earlier. My name was given to me by my father's father, my now deceased grandfather Paul Florence II. My grandfather passed the name down to me by inspiration of a man he had met while working in the military named Victor.

My grandfather described the man as joyous and free-spirited although it seemed that he had been nothing more but a mere victim of life itself. The man spent his last years as a homeless widower wandering place to place in hopes of a shelter to rest his old weary bones and food to feed his exhausted, worn-out stomach. He had been permanently constrained to a wheelchair after suffering an atrocious bombing accident that had detached both of his legs, his right arm, and had nearly separated his entire abdomen from the rest of his upper body.

If his physical disabilities couldn't have made his life a struggle as it had already been, his wife lost interest in him after seeing her husband's new monstrous appearance. She often complained about having to take care of him, repeatedly mentally abused him, and told him how she should have married his wealthier brother instead. She would partake in physically abusing him by throwing scorching hot coffee on him; pushing him down the fleet of stairs; hiding his wheelchair, thus forcing him to crawl, further damaging his body; and by burning the last remaining part of his leg stubs with a spoon that she had dipped in boiling water.

His wife began having multiple affairs with men around their area and would even bring them home and engage in sexual activities in front of her husband. His wife's lovers would also physically assault Victor and even engage in conversations with his wife about how hideous he was. She had once brought a handicapped child back to the home that had been in the same incompetent condition as Victor, missing both of his legs and only having hideously amputated stumps as a result; and out of carnal frustration and wanting to receive some form of sexual arousal, she cut off the remaining portions of the child's legs and shoved the dead bleeding morsels of flesh down Victor's throat before sexually stimulating herself with the other shriveled fragments.

Victor put up with this for almost two decades before his wife committed suicide by putting a gun onto the roof of her mouth and literally blowing her brains out while Victor watched in deep consternation. Her last words were,

"I hope you know you caused this." After the death of his wife, Victor lost the apartment that he was living in while being unable to work due to his disabilities and sadly morphed into another homeless statistic. My grandfather helped him out as much as he could until Victor unexpectedly died from several open wound infections, stemming from his wife's physical abuse, and unbearable stress at the age of forty-two.

Despite all of what he endured, he still represented himself as a kind-hearted man, full of integrity and altruism. Victor portrayed himself as a religious man, and as often as he could, he would sit and lecture children about biblical morals. My grandfather told me he named me after this man to show me that no matter what life blessed me with or cursed me with, he still believed that I could and I Would come out just fine.

Being the only child of both of my parents, I guess it would be appropriate to say that I experienced a rather regular childhood and that I witnessed nothing more than the average child. My parents adjusted to the normal stereotypical family portrayed in the sitcoms. My father would be up and off to work by eight o'clock, and my mother would spend her time cleaning and preparing dinner for when my father got back in from work. My parents rarely engaged in arguments, and the household always gave off that peaceful feeling.

Though I couldn't find anything to complain about, I always felt something was missing, as if a piece of my life had been being neglected. Living in Tucson, Arizona, I would often spend my free time engaging in trivial sports or riding my bike with a couple of acquaintances, nothing out of the ordinary. I never seemed to excel in my academics either, just an average B or C student.

I believe my life began its downfall when I became twelve years old. My mother's mother, my distant yet beloved grandmother, had been admitted into a mental institution for brutally murdering my grandfather. She had decapitated him while he slept and spent days resting next to his headless corpse. She had even catered to the corpse, cooking his favorite meals and bringing them to him and growing enraged when he didn't eat it, eventually causing her to lance open her husband's dead stomach and scrape her food into the decayed hollow. Neighbors heard her talking and laughing with the corpse, and then the simple buffoonery and chuckling would no sooner evolve into high tension of screaming and cursing. The neighbors thought nothing of it as they had always heard them hassle one another, and hearing them have yet another altercation became so normal that they thought no more of it and barely even heard it anymore.

The authorities apprehended her after days had grown to weeks and the neighbors began complaining about a displeasing smell coming from her apartment. When the authorities barged into her apartment without notice, they found her sleeping next to her husband's headless body. The body had been covered in maggots and other various insects and the inbred parasites had already began eating the rotting flesh of the corpse. The apartment was filthy, covered in bugs and rodents, and it appeared that mold had found its way forming on the walls.

The officers arrested my grandmother to her dissatisfaction and investigated the apartment. There they found the decapitated head of my grandfather underneath the very bed that she had been sleeping in. The head looked to be far from just decayed, also covered in maggots and flies, and the officers sighted a gutted, mutilated rodent devouring the left eye. Loathsomely, the disemboweled rat was also missing its own eyes.

Disturbingly, upon further searching her apartment, authorities found several old photographs and portraits of my grandmother and grandfather, and in all the pictures, he is repulsively decapitated, despite that these pictures had been taken years prior to this gruesome incident. There had also been an unknown substance cemented onto my grandmother's feeble hands, and after being taken in for investigation, it arose that my grandmother had been sexually stimulating the corpse days after she had murdered her husband.

After almost two years of investigation, the death was ruled a homicide, and she was sentenced to spend the rest of her life in a mental institution just outside of Kansas. The death of my grandfather affected both my mother and me, my mother more so because she felt as if she had lost both of her parents.

My father decided that we go to Kansas and visit my grandmother to show her support. While there, we only received limited visitation with her due to the status of her mental health. She stayed in a pale white room with a small white table, and a white bed no bigger than a flat paper- board. My mother couldn't even bare to speak to her in such a state and just ended up leaving and returning to wait in the car.

My grandmother confided to both my father and me that she experienced sleep paralysis and had extreme, very graphic, night terrors of being raped by Satan. She told us that the dream would always start off the same; she'd appear in an abnormally dim abandoned cabin, stranded and having no idea how she had gotten there in the first place. The atmosphere would be cold and boisterous. A small, dusty window inside of the cabin would reveal that she had been confined in a wooded area surrounded by dead withering oak trees that danced horrendously in the wind. Glowering clouds would shroud the ink-like sky causing shredded guts of rain to begin pouring. The more she looked at the trees, the darker and thinner they became, growing extra branches which just grew weak and shriveled away.

While trying to search the room for a flashlight or a telephone to call someone, she looked in the corner of her eye only to find a small white child as young as maybe six or seven years old. The child appeared barefooted, and had oversized bright blue eyes and wore long pitch- black clothing. She described the child as always looking dejected, whimpering, or crying. She would approach the child, and the child's crying would grow louder. The child began mewling like a newborn, whining and wailing. Then the child's eyes suddenly became bloodshot, and the child was no longer crying tears, but streams of luminous blood, appearing similar to the vital fluid draining from the minced lacerations of a stab victim. She said when she saw this, she always backed away from the seemingly possessed bairn, and the child then raised his left hand, revealing a deep cut that looked to be the result of a knife, and in the cut contained a puddle of maggots; some dead, some alive. It became apparent that the child was growing angry.

At this point in the dream, she would panic and look for a way to exit the room, but she found herself unable to move and bound to a piece of wood that mounted itself on the wall of the cabin. As she struggled to free herself from the piece of wood, chains would appear on her hands and feet, and she soon found herself growing weak and impotent to even move around. She said the more she looked at the child, the more she slipped out of consciousness.

She believed that the child's stature began repulsively burgeoning; his limbs stretched out across the room outlandishly as he hovered over her, breaking from out of his clothing and revealing his nude repugnant body. His body lacked pieces of flesh, revealing several of his rotted internal organs, and his body was covered in multiple stab wounds. The child's complexion went from white to a pale green and his eyes from baby blue to a dark burgundy. His face grew longer like that of an aardvark, and his nose fell off, revealing two tiny black holes full of parasites. His face started deforming itself, raising one of his eyes and lowering the other one to his chin area. The eye that raised itself popped and the residue splattered on her face. Thin, sepia colored horns that looked like the piece of wood that she was bound to extended from out of the top of his blemished skull. The child no longer looked like a child, but an anomalously tall, grotesquely deformed, unidentified creature.

The creature then violently raped her, and portions of its face began to fall off, eventually melting away and leaving nothing but blood and small pieces of flesh on the side. Although the creature no longer had a face, it managed to form a lingering mouth, and when it opened its mouth, she heard what she believed to be the sound of schoolchildren laughing and playing on a playground, which slowly developed into sounds of pain and agony, the schoolchildren being ripped apart and murdered one by one.

She closed her eyes, and when she opened them she was surrounded by numerous demons, all of them being as black as coal and just as tall and thin as the creature raping her. They all appeared to be covered in eyes, all of them blinking, which soon became bloodshot. As the creature whom she identified as Satan continued to fiercely rape her, the skin on the side of its face stretches and pieces itself back together, revealing the face of her deceased husband. After she would see the face of her husband, she would wake up, only to find herself in bed staring at her pale ceiling. She had been having these dreams for the past month, and she had told the staff and even her own personal psychologist, but they all disregarded her claims and concluded that she had an overactive imagination and wanted nothing more but attention.

A couple of weeks later, following our visit, my mother received a call in the morning from the psychiatric ward. It was reported that my grandmother had killed herself with a weapon she had somehow managed to steal from the cafeteria in the hospital's kitchen. She was found laid across her bed with her intestines in her hands.

3

. . . .

When my mother learned that her mother had killed herself while incarcerated, she stood still like a plastic dummy, shaking her head in deep denial and rejecting any and everything the hospital staff told her that had occurred. She stood completely silent, as though her thought pattern had frozen, and she couldn't think of the exact words to say.

Although her frame stood still, her eyes made way around the kitchen in a timorous manner. She began trembling as if she had been caught in a blizzard, and her right hand began to twitch uncontrollably. As the staff member continued to unsuccessfully inform her about my grandmother's death, my mother began making an insufferable shrieking noise. She sounded like a two-month-old puppy that had been left to fend for itself in the rain. For all the years that I had seen my mother distressed, I must say that this could have been the worst position she had ever been in. Her face got whiter than it had already been, as if a demonic spirit had engulfed her soul and left her lifeless body standing with no further consequent.

My mother finally seemed to gain awareness of her surrounding and managed to pull herself together and snap out of her mental confinement. She received full control of her body once more and contained her right hand from shuddering any longer. My mother took a small, very brief and unenthusiastic sigh and began speaking into the phone, finally responding to the woman who had been unfortunate enough to relay the invidious news.

If telling someone that their mother had committed suicide and had been found in the most ghastly of all forms couldn't have been horrid enough, the staff member felt the need to go into detail about how my grandmother had committed suicide and how the staff had discovered her expired.

According to the woman passing along the message, after eating dinner and being left unattended by supervisors, my grandmother had nonchalantly walked into the cafeteria and picked up a butcher knife. She hid the butcher knife in her vaginal region, and afterward the callous staff members escorted her back to her room, unaware that she had gained access to a weapon. That night, when she began having the same nightmare about being raped by Satan, a loud dreadful scream came from her room repeatedly until the staff made their way to find the culprit of the repulsive screeching. Apparently, hearing my grandmother scream in her sleep had become a regular occurrence for the hospital staff in which they had been ignoring for the past three months, but this scream struck their attention to the point that they felt something had gone terribly wrong. When they opened the door to her room, the view was appalling. My grandmother was stretched flat across her bed, having had cut deeply into her stomach with the butcher knife, slicing open her stomach and pulling out her intestines and removing her entrails. Her entrails were laid out across the bed, and blood had been leaking out of her exposed stomach onto the bed and dripping down to the floor.

She had ripped out her colon and several of her important tissues, and all were planted across the room, staining the walls with blood and portions of her mutilated organs. The knife had been driven so far into my grandmother's stomach that it had gotten tangled in with her intestines, and the inexperienced staff had to go into her stomach to remove it, resorting to cutting her intestines off with other knives that they had acquired from the cafeteria kitchen.

While operating on the elderly woman, severing her insides with the jagged trenchant, they found to their displeasure that she was not dead. My grandmother blinked, and suddenly began screaming in profound torment. She hissed like an angry feline and expressed the anguish she was experiencing through her green pupils. She began hallucinating and cursing at the staff. The staff was unable to make out what she was trying to say, other than, "Why are you doing this to me, Paul? I killed you. Why are you messing with me? You're dead. Leave me alone for Christ's sake!"

After those very words, my grandmother had died, losing entirely too much blood and oxygen. The staff managed to remove the knife from her insides, the majority of which, she had tightly gripped in her palms. To their antagonizing shock, when they removed some of her entrails that had glued themselves to the wall, there they noticed a stain of blood that spelled "wodaeM elttiL" ("Little Meadow" backward). Little Meadow was a nickname given to my grandmother by my grandfather, describing her vibrant green eyes. He was the only one who called her by that name.

4

. . . .

t took my mother a few seconds to fully absorb the news
she had just obtained. She broke down in the middle of
the kitchen floor and began sobbing insanely. My father
heard her while sitting in the living room watching the
television, and he ran into the kitchen to her comfort. He
tried to understand what exactly had happened, only
receiving bits and pieces of the story. It was almost as if my
mother had lost her tongue. She could no longer speak. She
just laid on the tan-tiled floor sobbing, tears running down
her face like the rain water on a car window. My father
hated it when my mother cried, and every time she had a
fit, rather it be necessary or not, he tried to repair it to the
best of his abilities.

My mother wouldn't look up to my father; she just buried her head in between her arms and continued weeping.
"Lauren," my father called sympathetically to my mother.
She refused to reply. My father picked my mother up and
held her in his arms as she continued bewailing. She had
a monumental amount of tears flowing from her eyes, and

her black mascara began to melt, dripping down her cheeks like wet black paint on a dry wall.

My mother struggled trying to speak. She sounded like a toddler, slurring words and trying to pronounce her sentences. She sounded foreign. The way my mother held onto my father in such a demeanor of helplessness and need and hassled to get one word out showed that she was in deep tribulation beyond any sort of repair. As my father held my mother in concerning amenity, he noticed the phone hanging off the hook, and finally taking this morbid ordeal into full consideration, he made himself able to hear a person speaking on the other line. My father automatically concluded that my mother's sadness had more than likely derived from something that she had heard on the telephone.

My father placed my grieving mother down gently on the tile and without hesitation, picked up the phone and introduced himself. He immediately realized that it was the psychiatric ward that my grandmother had been staying at. My father introduced himself as Ronald Florence, the husband of Lauren Florence and son-in-law of Susan Grace. The hospital staff informed my father that his mother-in-law had committed suicide the night before by cutting open her stomach with a butcher knife and spreading the insides of her abdominal region across the room. The woman told him that the staff went to retrieve the knife from her stomach, only to wind up slicing her intestines apart from her accessible stomach, unenlightened that she was still alive and had been fully awake.

My father had no other emotion to express at the time but to be truly repelled by what he had heard. Just thinking that someone had butchered themselves up and been operated on with full awareness had made him sick to his stomach. My father felt compassion for my grandmother, for he knew that she was a sick woman in need of help, and the very hospital that had promised to fulfill those aids had betrayed her without a doubt. My father then turned and looked at my daunting mother, who had now picked herself up from the floor and wiped the tears away from the bottom of her eyes.

Although it looked like she felt better, she still stood there in total shock. My mother looked lost, like a small child who had lost her mother in a grocery store. My father asked the woman on the phone if it was possible to access her body so they could give her a proper burial. The woman said that the way my grandmother looked after she died, it would be almost unrecognizable to even claim her as our own. Her tan skin had morphed into an Alice blue, looking like the mold on stale food. Her body had stiffened, as hard as dry clay, and her stomach had been so mutilated that it was almost impossible to put her intestines back inside. They just hung outside of her open stomach, disintegrating. She said that the mortification of my grandmother's insides had been made visible, showing the last remaining of her tissues slowly wasting away into hard gray matter that stunk like hell. Her fingernails turned into a yellowish green, looking like rotten spinach, and her fingers turned black; some of them had already fallen off. Her stomach acid was completely macroscopic, and it had discharged all over her body, spilling down to her decayed feet.

To my father's strong censure, the staff member then revealed that the hospital had already disposed of my grandmother's body and had had her cremated, concluding that she was an "old nut" and "no one would have wanted her old evil worthless ass anyway." She said my grandmother's cadaver took up a substantial amount of space, and needed to be removed as required by law. My father held back from relieving any expression of anger as he had seen my mother's condition as it had already been and didn't want to make anything worse.

I received the news severely, but not to the extent that my mother and father had acquired it. Losing my grandmother had been very difficult, especially on my mother. She became withdrawn from the family for a few years, neglecting my father and me and abandoning her old cheerful behavior. My father became depressed due to the neglect that my mother had strained on him because of her difficulty coping. My mother began taking prescription medication in order to deal with her severe depression, the treatment causing her to experience horrific and eerie nightmares in which she would discover revoltingly burned and sliced open yet functioning limbs throughout the home, all of them belonging to my deceased grandmother. Sometimes, my mother would awaken in the middle of the night and view what appeared to have been her mother's rotted appendages gruesomely stitched onto her body, her own limbs butchered off and thrown into the corner in bloody, mutilated chunks.

When I became fifteen years old, I can say that that's when things began to go back to normal. My mother found helpful coping strategies in counseling, and she and my father began to rebuild the relationship that they had once lost. No sooner after that, my parents began having discussions about expanding the family. The household was finally at peace again. On the night following my father's forty-fifth birthday, a masked intruder found their way into the house and opened the door to my parents' bedroom. Without my knowledge, the person had only been in the house for not even ten minutes, and I assumed that my mind had been playing tricks on me as I always seem to see strange shadows moving in the dusk. When morning approached, my father was found alive but his face horribly disfigured. My mother was found dead; her stomach slashed open with an unknown object. She was four months pregnant.

5

. . . .

f I could describe my mental state at the time when I had viewed my mother's crisp contracted body that morning, I'd say nothing but black and white. My mind had gone far from any describable colors, for I now felt the true meaning of loss and pain. I couldn't think of anything worse for a child to witness than the view of their treasured mother's mangled corpse lying in front of their very eyes. I felt weak, defenseless. Looking into my mother's dead eyes knowing that I could do nothing to help her concealed me with an enormous amount of disrepute.

I hated myself, but for the wrong reason. Being a child as young as fifteen years old, I guess I didn't know how I should feel. Anger had to have been a copious emotion at the time. My left eye searched for a befitting tear to lend me while I prospected my last view of my mother. I couldn't bring myself to fully cry tears. I just stood there, in a lumbering position, staring at my dead mother. The intruder had lacerated her stomach completely open with what looked to be a wooden dagger. I could rightfully make that assumption because I could clearly see scanty pieces of wood as small as an ant, stabbed around the flesh of my mother's open stomach. The killer had stabbed her in the stomach with this piece of wood and somehow dug into her skin and carved a flap, lifting it up and gaining a passageway inside.

My mother had also been stabbed in the throat horrifically, and the killer didn't even think to spare her the agonizing discomfort of pain. She had missing fragments of skin around her neck, and I could see several lines of luminous pink flesh, which was now covered in drying blood, implying that the killer had sliced her neck with the dagger, peeling off pieces of her skin. Some of the sliced skin on her neck had been positioned upward, revealing the inside flesh of her neck.

I had been studying the deficiencies of my mother that I hadn't even cared to take time and notice the big picture: my mother no longer had a baby in her stomach. The person who murdered her had removed the baby from the inside of her and did God only knows what with it. A pool of blood surrounded my mother's stomach area, including the pieces of wood that stood deeply engraved in her skin. I wanted to vomit, but I held my urge, in respect of my mother.

When it became clear to me that my mother had been murdered and the person who committed the gruesome act separated the baby from her, a cloud of conniption swept me like a violent hurricane. I grew enraged and dropped down to my knees and moved closer to my mother. I had an outbreak of tears branch from both my eyes as I laid there on the floor of my parents' bedroom, looking into the pale face of my mother. I couldn't hold them back any longer. I put my hand on my mother's frigid face, and I rubbed my hand back and forth, in blundering hopes of somehow bringing her back. Her face felt like I had stuck my hand into a freezer or as if I had dipped them into a lake from Antarctica. She didn't even feel human anymore. As I continued to cry, my nose began to run, and I withdrew the mucus back into my nose repeatedly and kissed my mother on the cheek.

I pulled the red cover from over the body of my unconscious father, and I was absolutely perturbed. What was I looking at? Was that even my father, the man who raised me from an infant anymore? I felt as though I had literally begun dancing with The Devil. Out of exasperation, I threw my fists down on my parents' bed and began cursing God. I shouted as loud as I could, spewing anything blasphemous that my mind could conjure up. What the hell did I do to deserve this? First, my grandmother slaughtered my grandfather and then committed suicide while in a mental institution; then my childbearing mother was murdered in her sleep by some sick bastard?

"Damn God!" Yes, those were the words that I yelped that morning. I was not proud of it. Not at all. I didn't know what to do with myself after observing my mother's lifeless body. No one would want to see their mother's stomach gashed open. No one in their right mind. No one would want to know that some maniac had gashed her stomach open and removed their soon-to-be brother or sister either. No one in their right mind. I had seen all of this, being a kid myself. Fifteen years old.

The crimes went unsolved. My father never seemed to be the same again either. He became a hermit, so ashamed to go out into the world in fear that he would be shunned. Though my father had been alive, he might as well have been dead, for his body had become nothing more but a flesh-covered casket.

I never stopped my mind from wondering, "What if." What if my mother hadn't been murdered that night. What if my mother had went on to give birth and introduce my baby brother or sister into the world. What if my father hadn't been disfigured and hadn't drifted off into his Own world. Every time my mind started to think, I just got sad and turned it off, like a television channel in which you find no interest in. I now know how my mother felt when she received the bereaving news about my grandmother. If only I knew how to be supportive at that time. She sure did need it, like I needed it at this moment. As I got older, my soul formed into a white plastic bag, just floating around in the wind, seeking a place to find unity.

6

. . . .

No matter how older and wiser I became, I can truthfully say that I never fully recovered from the death of my mother. The view of her hideously violated corpse firmly attached itself to my mind, like wet gum on the bottom of someone's shoe. My mother's ravaged remains danced in my head disturbingly. Her stomach would slice itself open with an impalpable entity and an unseen, almost invisible, perpetrator would reach into her stomach, pull the baby out, and afterward stitch her stomach back together with false sewing materials such as spiked wooden stitches, only to end up slicing it open once more and repeating the same exact routine. I would be forced to stand in the corner while this wickedness occurred, listening to her cries for mercy and benevolence. I called for my mother, but she couldn't respond; she just screamed in an execrable tone as she watched in plenary loathsome as the invisible beast continued to slash open her stomach and remove her baby. These visions would flash in my head as I lay awake in the night with my eyes closed, in desperate hopes of falling asleep. When these grisly terrors entered into my mind, I would often leave my bedroom and pour myself a glass of water, abandoning my need for sleep and making a home in the kitchen or living room.

Right after her death, I began to have frequent dreams about my mother, reminiscing about being a small child and assisting her to bake pastries in the kitchen. In those dreams, a younger version of myself, approximately five or six years old, would be standing in the kitchen stirring cake mix next to my mother, having a jubilant conversation about the activities I participated in while at elementary school. The discussions we had were always innocent and calming, setting a warm and comforting tone to the scenery of the kitchen and providing my subconscious peace and relaxation. The sun would always beam through the small square window in the kitchen, further enhancing the harmonious mood and arranging a satisfying view of the setting.

My mother and I would revel around the kitchen, splashing cake mix onto each other and making an unnecessary mess out of the kitchen counter with our careless antics. After my mother put the cake into the oven, she would become concerningly silent. She unnaturally stood in front of the oven with her brown eyes seemingly glued onto the dusky black stove, positioning herself into an odd, almost satanic form. My mother stood perfectly still, staring at the stove as if she were watching her child play on a swing set. While still staring at the stove, my mother addressed that she had a secret she would like to tell me and sternly remarked not to mention it to my father. My mother's feminine high-pitched voice sank deeper to a more confident masculine voice, leading her to eventually develop a solid Adam's apple, which consolidates the more it expanded. My mother's pale skin began to glitch, like a computer software game or like the static on an out-of-service television channel.

Noticing the sudden changes in my mother's appearance didn't seem to upset me or spark my attention for some reason, and I unwittingly agreed not to tell my father the secret she had for me. My mother then turned forward facing me, displaying her stomach, revealing that she was pregnant. She stared at me in deep disorientation.

By this time in the dream, the elegant sunlight had faded away into nothing but blackness, and I could see the shaded clouds morphing together and composing a light drizzle, which eventually progressed into a riotous thunderstorm. The windows began to frantically crack, and the kitchen window in which we were standing next to broke violently, causing the glass to shoot onto the kitchen floor in large parcels.

I expressed excitement and showed lively astoundment when I discovered that my mother was pregnant, and I asked her if she knew whether it was going to be a boy or girl. My mother's stomach was bulging, and it looked like she could have given birth at any minute. I could see small feet kicking inside of her stomach unpleasantly, gruesomely scratching and tearing the outer layer of her abdomen, and I asked her if she was going to go into labor, in which she responded, "Yes."

I was jaunty about the situation, cheering and jumping up and down eagerly, until she harshly informed me that the occasion is not to be celebrated. I asked my mother why and managed to ask her why I couldn't apprise my father on the situation. She then told me that the reason I couldn't tell my father was because it was not his baby. She cheated on him. With Satan. Her voice was then overpowered by the sounds of the clamorous thunderstorm.

My mother reached down onto the kitchen floor and picked up a long piece of glass. She then removed her dress, stripping partially nude, and proceeded to cut a thin line across her stomach, opening it and allowing the baby to fall out. The baby was small, wrinkly, and an unhealthy light blue, and to my bewilderment, the baby grew into a full adult, still blue and disgustingly wrinkled. My mother was greatly disconcerted that the baby made it into a full adult, and out of anger, she grabbed the now adult child by the head and forced it into the garbage disposal. She cut its head off and left its body lying bleeding on the kitchen floor.

My mother then opened the door to the oven to check on the baking cake, only to find the adult child's decapitated head in its place. She then began chuckling in an abnormally grim manner, going on to entice me to rape the burned flesh off my dead sibling.

After that, I found the strength to wake myself up from this horrid dream and just look into my dark closet, trembling and praying for morning to find its way sooner. I didn't even think about telling my father about these dreams and getting help. He was already long gone and needed help himself, so I knew he didn't have the competency to help me. Since my father had become a hermit, he ended up quitting his job at the gas company and just habituated to making a living off my mother's inheritance he had gained from her insurance.

When I became sixteen years old, my father sent me to live with his mother and father, my grandparents, in Houston, Texas, hoping that by doing so I'd have a better life than I would by continuing to live with him.

I was staying with them for two weeks then when my grandparents received a call from the fire department and police station, asking if Ronald Florence happened to be their son. My father had jumped off a bridge onto the freeway, landing face flat before being lacerated open by multiple vehicles. He was found with a ripped picture of my mother and me in both of his hands, a picture of me in his right and a picture of her in his left. His body burst the moment he landed.

7
. . . .

The first person who divulged to me about what had happened to my father had been my grandmother, after an officer had enumerated the information to her on the telephone. The anguish stricken in my grandmother's gracefully aged blue eyes flooded her with undefinable hurt as she forwarded to me what the officer had notified her on.

My father had eradicated himself by aberrantly plunging onto a freeway roughly, causing his heavily weighted body to shatter like a glutted water balloon, dispatching vast amounts of blood onto the brimming highway and defiling the streets with chunks of his flesh. The entire freeway had been concealed in my father's blood, and portions of his flesh even flew off his body, landing on windshields and abundantly staining passing automobiles. Vehicles unintentionally drove over my father's torn flesh, which resulted in car accidents and several injuries and deaths.

My father's battered limbs had been withdrawn from his body, and his whole arm made its way onto a window of a moving school bus, startling many of the children on the bus and frightening some of them to the point that they died the moment they witnessed the traumatic event. Watching a man's body demolish had taken an unfavorable effect on the children viewing it, and the kids who had been lucky enough to live through the nightmare may have possibly been traumatized for the rest of their lives.

Not only had my father taken his life, but he also stripped the lives from many innocent children, including the few who were still alive. What a calamity, a freeway full of the scattered remains of a suicide victim, totaled cars, and an entire school bus of dead children.

Upon learning that my father had taken his own life, a malicious paramount planted itself into my brain and dominated my mind, convincing me that killing myself would be the only way to finally emancipate me from this psychological excruciation that had been savagely haunting me continuously. I heard a stygian voice that sounded like it had been in immense dolor murmur in mind, "Do it for me."

The voice told me to walk into the kitchen, pull a knife out of the drawer, and rend my throat open. The voice tried to convince me that by ripping open my throat, I'd finally be ending my pain and putting a stop to any future anguish, sending me directly to hell to be with my father.

I refused to slash my own throat, thus making the voice in my head angry with me. I suddenly lost contact with reality, and my grandparents' living room immediately faded into gray nothingness. An emaciated figure with a livid colored hood appeared in front of me, gradually slithering closer to my still body. I could not see the figure's face, for it had been completely varnished in its hood, and its clothing made it appear almost defunctive. Its hands were covered in maroon blood that dripped like the tiny specs of water from a faucet, and looking closer underneath the blood, I could clearly see goldenrod-colored perished bones.

The figure then told me to kill myself and handed me a black dagger. It had such an unsettling voice, comparable to glass being shattered in my ear. It laughed faintly and told me to press the dagger against my throat and cut and continue cutting until the figure directed me to stop. I infuriatingly shouted at the figure, refusing to cut my throat. This upset it. The figure told me to do it for my father and my mother, and at that point it attempted to shove the dagger into my hands. I rejected the dagger.

The figure then pulled over its hood, revealing both the head of my mother and father hideously joined together on the figure's single body. The figure does not have a face, other than the heads of my parents. The heads of my mother and father were obviously lifeless as they were a blanched green, and I could see them decomposing.

My body began to frantically shake as I stood in front of the beast in ample discomfort, and then it raised its hand

and sliced my father's throat with the dagger. A large leakage of blood dripped from my father's open neck, and then the figure cut my mother's throat. As a drizzle of blood poured from my mother's neck, the figure's hand forced my mother's mouth open and pulled out her tongue, causing her to cough up an undeveloped baby arm, which fell to the ground and crawled underneath the figure's black robe. My father's decayed head began speaking to me, telling me in a dejected voice that I had the chance to spend eternity in hell with him, but I refused. My father's eyes rolled into the back of his head leisurely, and when they roll back, I see dark, clammy blood that read, "So long, son," spread across my father's dead, white eyeballs. His speech no sooner became muffled and slowly faded away into the sound of screeching static.

As the sound of static drifted into my ears, I found myself looking into the ocean-blue eyes of my grandmother, who had been telling me about my father's death the entire time. She asked me what had caused me to start trembling, and I simply told her, "The thought of Death."

For some reason, the death of my father had not affected me like the death of my mother had, and at his funeral, I shed no tears. I may have felt this way due to the person my father became toward the end of his life. My father grew distant and expelled himself from being any sort of parenting figure in my life. He became less concerned with my schoolwork and failed to teach me certain lessons as I grew to become a young man. He stayed isolated in the odious, tenebrous attic, writing short stories and poems with notebook paper and pens he had me pick up for him after I had gotten out of school.

I can recall once asking him what he found so interesting to write about in those notebooks in which he replied, "Plans for next year."

I can candidly say that toward the end of my father's life, he became a very sick man. Without his knowledge, I had arrived home from school earlier than usual one afternoon and discovered my father masturbating fervidly in the bathroom to a picture of my dead mother. The picture had been taken the next morning after my mother's murder by crime scene investigators, and somehow my father had gotten ahold of a few of the photographs. How could my father do such a thing, to a picture of his wife's marred corpse?

The following night, when my father had gone to sleep, I snuck into the attic and went through a stack of papers he had folded on a desk. There I found several pictures of my mother's dead body, and inadvertently, I stumbled upon pictures of my grandmother's corpse. Plausibly, the mental institution my grandmother stayed at also had detectives come in and take crime scene photos as part of an investigation, and the hospital sent some of the photos to my parents, in which my father never presented to my mother but instead held onto them himself. I could only imagine his true purpose for keeping those photos. I spotted the notebooks on his desk and decided to take a look inside of them to find what he had been writing while confined into the attic every day. I found nothing but blank pages.

To this day, I still reflect on my father's response.

8

. . . .

My father's funeral fell on a grody, somber Sunday morning on the first of November. As my grandmother and grandfather prepared to get dressed for the services, I stepped outside unnoticed onto the ligneous porch to sit alone and take into regard all the horrors that had occurred in such a short period of time and to hopefully regain my mental stability.

To my disillusion, I had walked into a distressing ordeal, viewing the inanimate reality of what had been left of the once ecstatic environment. The skies emerged into a faint gamboge color, looking bedraggled and savagely tattered, like a rusted dilapidated pickup truck, and strips of ailing swarthy markings similar to tire streaks, wrapped them horridly. Vigorous sorrow overwhelmed me and negatively affected my mood as I examined the glum blemishes crookedly painted across the repellent heavens. The drabby clouds hung in an awry manner and scattered themselves across the small comfortless city, appearing thinner and sickly the further they haltingly dragged themselves apart into the forlorn of the nonexistent firmament. I suggested that something must have been robustly faulty, seeing that the sky looked like an infernal oil painting, but I disregarded my gut feelings as I continued to perceive this distorted world.

Inspecting my contorted surroundings, it became obvious that all the town's trees had died and had been left to dissolve into nothing more but vile, sooty elongate sticks that stood slumped over and tilted, which eventually found the strength to sway sluggishly and make a detestable bawling noise, sounding like a feeble newborn being ruthlessly suffocated to death. The atmosphere felt boldly bleary and mentally prostrated, somehow managing to match my darkened emotions at the time.

Although I had made myself isolated and secluded, a fanciful substance arose in my train of thought and told me that something was wrong and to get out of there as soon as I could. *Get out of what?* I thought to myself. Before gaining the chance to rely on what had been told to me, I heard a raucous shrill beam into my ears. The vexatious noise amplified horrifically and began rooting into something deeper as though a demented speaker or surround sound had been shoved heedlessly into my eardrums. Anticipating to expel the harrowing sound, I turned toward the direction of the screeching, only to see my neighbor murdering his wife on his murky lawn. She had been stripped nude after attempting to haul him off her, in which he uses this to his twisted advantage. He tied her ripped, faded yellow dress around her neck tightly, cutting off her oxygen and causing blood to flow from her frangible neck like the streams in a mountain, silencing her cries for mercy as he uncontrollably pounds an unyielding stone into her skull, paying no mind to the tides of blood draining from her head.

As he continued to beat the stone into her head, I began to hear sounds of her skull cracking; eventually smashing, in which she let out a delicate shriek, finally dying. He used the rock to purge the skin off her head, before shoving the stone into her skull. I then noticed a group of neighbors surrounding him, disturbingly watching him nonchalantly as he finished murdering his wife. Frightfully, none of these people had faces. Just white voids. These people appeared to have human hands, being the color of the average Caucasian person, just a dimmer shade. Their heads slightly tilted side to side in a morbid manner as they looked down on the man. He then took his wife and crammed her into a dead tree stump, and I noticed the neighbors gathering around, undressing themselves, preparing to rape her.

After witnessing such a scourge, I hastily sprint back into my grandparents' home to begin getting myself together. As I walked into the lurid, archaic enclosing of my grand-parents' residence, I found my grandmother sitting acutely on the side of her bed with her head thoroughly slumped down to her knees. She was facing one of the four walls in her room, and her blinds were completely sealed, making her room aphotic and hard to move around in. My grandmother's shoulders moved up and down inactively, and I heard her thinly weeping.

I hesitated to walk closer to my grandmother, gaining morale, in which I did. I ask her pleasantly what was the matter and if she would like to talk about it. My grandmother ignored me and buried her head further into her lap. I stared at her for a brief moment before looking over her shoulder, realizing that she was sobbing at a photograph of my dismembered father. I could see that the photo had been taken on the highway just minutes after the accident as my father no longer had his arm attached and his entire chest and stomach had been torn open. She had her eyes focused on the flesh in the background, which had shot off of him. The photo had also captured eerie snaps of the car accidents that were involved in the incident, including part of the school bus that several children had died on, the rest of the half being cut out due to the length of the picture.

Looking closer, I could see the unnatural expression on the face of one of the children as he watched my father's severed arm paste itself onto the moving bus. It appeared that the camera had shot the child dying as I could make out what looked to be the child's spirit releasing itself from the body, looking similar to steam arising from a searing dish.

My grandmother rubbed her corrugated fingers on the picture as she continued mourning. I told my grandmother compassionately that I knew what was going on was horrible, but my father was now in a better place. I tried to lighten her disposition and encouraged her to put on proper clothing, seeing that she only had on a shabby gown full of holes and burly tears. She was sitting with her back turned to me, but then her head alarmingly rotated to face me as I stood over her. My grandmother's head was larger than usual, looking similar to an inflated pumpkin with skewed edges. Her eyes were bloodshot, and her left pupil had drifted into the back of her eyelid where it was no longer visible.

"What's going on is horrible?" my grandmother asked me as if she was in shock. She then formed a broad, horrendous smile across her face, causing the skin on her dry lips to swiftly crack, shattering away into small bloody pieces. "Your father is dead. Your father is dead. My son is dead. This is something to celebrate, Victor. Lucifer always comes around. We all know your father was sick anyway, being a necrophiliac and all. Yes, he's been that way since he was a boy, as young as you. Oh, how we had to keep him from drooling over the casket at his great-grandmother's funeral." Not knowing how to respond, I left my grandmother's room and came in contact with my grandfather. My grand-father pointed for us to walk out of the door in a predominant manner. My grandfather was dressed in a brown suit. He had on black dress shoes and a black and mahogany tie. He seems to pay no attention to my grandmother and me not being dressed appropriately. When my grandfather opened the front door to lead us out, we saw a supposed dead dog lying slanted on our doorstep.

The dog was meager and brown, and its lower half was separated from its upper half. The dog's fur was matted, and some of it appeared to have been ripped out. The portions that were ripped out reveal the dog's skin, which consisted of hideous open scars, similar to that of a person who had just undergone surgery. Most of the dog's stitches were sewen together adequately, the majority bare and exposed. The dog's paws were sliced open, and its paws and lower half were bleeding tremendously. Its eyes were thoroughly red as if they were painfully blistering, and the dog was cross-eyed.

My grandmother walked over to the dog. The dog lifted its head up torpidly and groaned in an abysmal voice, "Help me." My grandfather became enraged at the dog, shouting at it to "Shut the fuck up," before stepping on it, crushing its head briskly. Although the dog's head was now smashed, a dismal voice was heard coming from the dog's head, which sounded like gibberish, being that the dog's words were now being reversed.

My grandfather wiped his shoes across the colorless grass, in attempts to rid the dog's blood, and he unlocked the door to his burnt umber Cadillac. The windows were broken out, but my grandfather said nothing of this. Once my grandmother and I got into the car, my grandfather started the engine and began driving backward. As my grandfather drove, the dun roads suddenly disappeared, and he began driving in fog, causing the car to lift up and float into nothingness. While being in the car, I notice that my grandmother's head drastically reduced in size, going back to its regular capacity, but her eyes still remain bloodshot, looking caustic, and her left pupil is still hidden.

A heavy rain approached, and my grandfather let down the top of his car, concluding that he needed some "fresh air." Rain inundated over our heads, and they ignored the torrent completely and sat deathly still, glued to the seats of the car. As we approached the church, the rain let up to some small extent, and we walked into the deathly denomination. We were greeted tepidly by a few family members since we have a relatively small family. All our family was dressed in black, and several of them were wearing timber wolf–colored gloves. My grandparents and I sat next to our family, and to my utter loathing, I noticed that my father's funeral was an open casket.

As we sat and waited for the pastor to arrive, we were immersed with a dull, funereal tune played by the church's musician on a piano. The church's musician was a dark, tan man, looking as if his skin had been burned in an accident, and he was runty in size. I noticed that he did not have hands; he was using small deformed stubs to tap the keys on the piano. My family stiffly swayed to the tune, looking straight and appearing as if they are concentrating on something that wasn't there.

The pastor then walked into the room holding an already bloody bayonet, which he uses to cut the musician's stubs off with, causing the musician to drop underneath the piano as blood floods from his limbs. The pastor was a slim man, dressed in black as well. He was bald and had nothing more to his face but a mouth. He was missing eyes. The pastor began preaching immediately, yipping about my father burning in hell. The pastor then became unable for me to understand as he starts speaking in another language, a language that does not even exist. Once the pastor finished preaching, he was about to exit the room when my aunt spouts out, "What about the dance?"

My family became visibly eager and awaited for the event. The pastor then walked over to my father's casket and pulled his body out. My father's body was rotten and noxious, and his skin was white and sullen. His eyes are mashed into his head. My father's limbs were still detached, and several of his skin tissues were still gone, his last remaining skin rotting away. My family stood up and walked to the front of the church and began dancing with my father's body. Skin began to slide off his face and drop off his body as they glided around holding him.

My grandmother caressed what was left of my father's feculent lips. As she pulled her mouth away, it was veiled in a clan of leech, which without delay, masticated her tongue. I sat on an old defective seat in the back of the church as I watched this. My family turned to me and asked me to join them.

The musician's disjoined stubs arose and began pressing the keys on the piano, staining the keys with blood while playing a watered-down melody, playing more and more intensely as my family urged me to dance with my father. I look away from them, hoping to dampen the tension so they would leave me be, and I saw my mother's corpse sitting next to me. Her corpse was unattired, her stomach split open, revealing a hanging dead baby poorly attached to the inside. She no longer had a face, just a slivered skull. Despite her no longer having a face, my mother still had her attentive brown eyes. At first, I believed my mother was dead until she puts her putrescent hand on my shoulder and muttered in her usual voice, "Do it, Victor. Beelzebub loves a good dance. We will all be reunited in hell one day where we will do nothing but dance for him. Dance for Satan. He loves you."

I turned away from my mother and glimpsed into the face of my deceased father; and he boorishly smiled at me.

I awakened in the spare bedroom that my grandparents prepared for me, realizing that this was just a surrealistic dream. Just a sick, surrealistic dream. Coming to the awareness that my father's funeral was the next morning, I knew that I must get some rest so I could be both mentally and physically equipped, so I said goodnight to my mother's tranquil corpse, adjusted the sheets over her algid head, and drifted back to sleep.

9

. . . .

Both my grandmother and grandfather began noticing a dire adjustment to my natural mirthful demeanor. Although they had not been a strong presence in my life from the day my mother had given birth to me, I could unwittingly speculate that by just being my biological grandparents, they could certainly identify something being wrong with me. My grandparents were accustomed to my body movements and my posture and certain steps I made as I impelled through the hallway and into the kitchen; that quickly grew instilled into their heads as soon as they accepted me into their home at the age of sixteen. My grandparents could already sense how my mood was going to develop and what could possibly transpire from it by just listening to my voice, ignoring the fact that the day had just scarcely begun.

My grandmother especially had a skill for doing this, being that she had once taken minor psychology courses in college as a young woman, which eventually lead to her meeting my grandfather. Despite the courses being so minimal, she still acquired some passable, useful knowledge about the human mind, which included detecting modifications in a person's characteristics.

Oftentimes while secluded in the privacy of my room drawing inartistic pictures of my mother and observing photographs taken of my parents and me, desiring to relive the moment of that former irenic family again, I would overhear my grandparents discussing the recent alteration of my inclination and expressing their worriment. Knowing that my closest and only family members may have been stressed because of my inability to let things go and move on to the future brought me great shame. I did not conform with the idea of someone being upset because of my personal complications, and at that time, it just didn't register that they only cared for me and just wanted what was best. More than often did I myself wonder what was wrong with me, and I felt cursed that my inadequacies had made me someone's burden.

I felt distant from my grandparents, like I didn't belong there, similar to the only black sheep in the herd. Perhaps my mental state just couldn't take putting on an artificial smile anymore, and it finally began to deteriorate, taking into full effect the crisis I had languished through, morosely absorbing reality in its harshest form. It's as if my mind had been wearing Cimmerian, dreary shades, and it had had enough and decided to remove them, opening itself to the view of the sun. The only thing was, there is nothing bright about coming to the realization that both of your parents are dead and that there is nothing you can do to change that wretched fact.

Though my grandparents considered the importance of my well-being beyond a doubt, they just didn't know where to start, for they could see that the convivial Victor, who had once been profoundly familiar, no longer existed, and that a masked, almost unrecognizable entity had taken its place. I loved talking to my grandfather whenever I had an issue about anything, no matter what subject, as he always knew the exact words to say, and his advice invariably helped me through the toughest of all situations. Unknowingly, my grandfather specialized in helping others. But he was no mental health professional. He could not diagnose me, nor could he doubtlessly deduce the root of the problem.

As time progressed, I became mentally drained as though a vacuum cleaner had imbibed all the exertion out of my brain and left nothing but an arid, forsaken gash. I became lethargic in my body language, repining with every step I managed to make, and compelling my hands to abide as I went to reach for a necessity. I lost complete interest in my physical appearance, something that is profusely anomalous of my character. Atop of my mental woes, my dreams began getting out of hand, eventually dominating my sleep, as they advanced into something distressingly disordered and concerningly realistic.

I once had a dream that I had been forced to watch my father's moldering corpse have sex with my mother's dead, debauched body, while their deceased, unborn baby sodomized my father. The umbilical cord was still attached to the baby, and it wrapped around my father's neck and back as the deceased child abused him. The baby had rotted to the point that all of its skin had turned into a blackish brown, and the skin on its face twisted itself like the water being wrung out from a towel, and its mouth and eyes had liquefied away as if it had suffered the effect of an adjacent candle. The baby's noisome head transformed into the head of a fiendish wolf, and it chewed off the dead flesh of my father's back, biting down on the festering bones of his back and ruminating his cartilage as my father's blood wept from its mouth. Abnormally, my father showed signs of pleasure as this occurred, and the wolf continued to bite deeper into his back, eventually revealing his entire skeleton, which was moss green and full of parasite-like creatures that painfully inhabited his insides. Frequently I would wake myself from these brooding illusions, only to discover that I was still dreaming.

I informed my grandmother about these dreams and my difficulty sleeping, and after discussing it over with my grandfather, she decided to take me to see a trained doc-

tor who majored in dream interpretation. The beginning
of my treatment went well; I began to adjust to the doctor
and disclose to him the subject matter of my dreams and
explain to him the situation of my late parents. He seemed
as though he were a genial elderly man, a confiding person full of sympathy and loyalty; and the more I discussed
with him, I began to grow fond of his neighborly attitude. I
addressed him by his Arabic name, Dr. Balus Muhammad,
although he insisted that I address him by just "Balus."
It appeared that I hovered over him, being that he must
have been only about five feet or so, and he had an ashen
protracted beard that hung from his face halfway down to
his chest. He had caliginous skin, and though he may have
been in his sixties, he had very few wrinkles. He wore thin
white glasses and spoke with a strong accent, making it
bothersome to understand some of his words at times.

Balus prescribed me medicine to help me cope with my
phantasms as well as my frame of mind and overall mood.
Although they caused me to be more somnolent, the pills
he gave me seemed to work, and overtime, my dreams settled down and became less unhallowed. I no longer felt
unease going to sleep, and my grandparents felt at peace
knowing that I had found peace.

Once the doctor and I commenced seeing each other
on more friendly terms, I can say he started showing
me a side of him that I greatly did not appreciate. Balus

began making sexual remarks toward my grandmother, oftentimes outwardly flirting with her. He would palpate my grandmother inappropriately, even going as far as to gape at her backside, seeming as though he had forgotten his surrounds. I expressed my discomfort with this, in which Balus responded as being ostensibly embarrassed, claiming that he had meant nothing by it. I saw a decrease in his deportment for weeks at a time before Balus invited my grandmother to go dining with him. My grandmother seemed astounded at first and then went on to tell him that she is happily married to my grandfather. Balus told her that it was nothing romantic, just a harmless "night out," and he suggested that she ask her husband to see if it would be acceptable. My grandfather does not mind my grandmother going out with this man as he has never been the controlling type, and in fact, he wished her a good night and told her to enjoy herself.

While at an extravagant, gaudy restaurant, my grandmother and Balus got off on a good start, and Balus ordered them both a glass of wine, persuading her to loosen up. My grandmother civilly denied the alcoholic beverage, concluding that she did not drink and wanted to prevent any possibility of making a fool of herself. Balus respected my grandmother's decision and asked the waiter to reclaim her glass of wine and replace it with a glass of water. Once the waiter brought back my grandmother's water, she and

Balus continued to talk to one another, having casual conversation and discussing marriage and certain life events. Balus revealed that he was not married, nor had he even been married. As my grandmother searched for the words to respond, her voice became undermined and obscure and eventually diminished. She lost the ability to hold on to her glass; she dropped it, causing it to spill over the table, and she collapsed onto the floor.

That night marked the last time my grandmother saw the daylights of the public. She never came home that night. My grandfather and I called the police repeatedly and filed several reports. We went to the police station many times a day as much as we were allowed. Various posters of my grandmother's picture and information had been hung around on trees, convenience stores, and mailboxes across the city.

After nearly a month, we received a call by authorities, claiming that they had located my grandmother and found out what had happened. Apparently, Balus had hired a waiter to defile my grandmother's drink with Rohypnol and had dragged her unconscious body into an alley, where he and foreign gang members whom he had been associated with took turns pitilessly raping her. Most of the gang members were in their early twenties; some of them were as young as fourteen years old.

After researching Balus's history and going over his legal information, detectives found that he was not even a licensed doctor, but a prison escapist who had been sentenced to death on ten counts of aggravated assault, including the rape of his own infant daughter. Because Balus was not a legitimate doctor, the authorities ran tests on me to see what exactly it was that he had been prescribing me. He had been giving me gamma hydroxybutyric acid. For some reason, it had had no major negative effect on my body. The reason the medicine seemed to help me cope with my dreams simply was because I did not remember them. I still had the same night terrors; they were just unclear as to when I woke up.

My grandmother's body had been found inside of the trunk of an old car. She had been stuffed into a black trash bag, and the majority of her bones had been broken, including her arms, her legs, her feet, and her neck. Her genitalia had been mutilated, looking slashed and gashed open as if a forceful object were used. Due to the results of forensic science, my grandmother had had her bones broken and had been stuffed into the trash bag while alive and had been abandoned to stifle to death. Strikingly, authorities located my grandmother in the back of a hearse. Incongruently, while on supposed medicine that would help me restrain my nightmares, my most hellish reverie had become my reality.

10

. . . .

After the atrocious murder of my esteemed grandmother, I eventuated becoming my own specimen due to both growing older and as a mechanism to vacate the nefarious domain that my mind had been holding me prisoner in, knowing that that was something my grandmother would have wanted me to do as both she and my grandfather affirmed that I had the potential to travel anywhere my heart could have possibly desired in life.

Developing into my own man and leading a successful fate is the least I could have done for my departed grandmother, for I knew that although she no longer inhabited the physical world, she still possessed a consequential part of my life as a prominent being spiritually. Venturing to cleanse my mind and dig myself up from my own grave was something undoubtedly essential for not only my grandmother but for myself additionally. I knew how it felt to watch my father mentally impair himself and go through his final days as a corpse with a heartbeat, and through stern determination, I disallowed myself from transitioning into such. As I had earlier confirmed, I didn't use to transcend academically; if anything, I did a sufficient amount of work just suitable enough to get through and pass, exemplifying the wonted child that sat in the back of the classroom, procrastinating completing any given assignments and partaking in conventional childlike behaviors such as spouting out evident amiss in attempts to be whimsical, constructing paper objects and ejecting them throughout the room, and passing notes when I perceived an unaware teacher.

This uncaring, fatuous attitude automatically changed parlously ensuing my grandmother had been discovered slaughtered and forcibly packed in a dolorous manner into a paltry trunk, making it difficult for her to breathe properly as she attempted to verbally writhe, responding to her fragmented bones that had been folded in diverse positions, making it more excruciating to cope as she died. I took my grandmother's throes and her abject circumstance and used it as a metaphor for the way I had been managing to carry on—feeling suffocated, confined, broken, and languid.

Though I had been moving about feeling enervated and emasculated, I was far from dead, for I knew that I had a purpose to fulfill in this defective, incurable world. Using my grandmother's death as a form of influential motivation to keep me striving for better in life, I acknowledged the significance of my education and began taking my schoolwork into consideration, inhumanely imposing myself to complete a prodigious supply of assignments, with a hopeful ambition of reaching anything above average.

Toward the deadline of high school, I spent an abundant amount of time envisioning an eventual career in a field that would most likely be both satisfying and mentally reasonable. I took into account that my grandmother originally had plans of becoming a psychologist in her youthful years, but she deliberately abandoned her passion once she began to form a family with my grandfather. Though she never expressed any lament or deplored over her thoughtful decision, she still held indisputable signs that made me conclude that she may have been somewhat wistful about not finishing her schooling by the way she lauded mental health doctors and how she always read books based on the studies of psychology.

My grandmother generally spoke to me about my future and attempted to open conversations based on occupations and perhaps going to college but sooner or later stopped, because I was too oblivious to even consider my future, and I always came up with a hindrance whenever the subject came up. Perchance, my tangled mind had been too busy trying to break free from the compacted web of contretemps that it had no room to supply to even care about a future, but that was no excuse.

I believe what altered my career choice and opened me up to this nonplussed world came from a highly religious

Catholic family that I used to live across from. The family consisted of three people, a man, his wife, and their bairn daughter, and they lived life as any other common family. The people had religious signs stationed in front of their yard, including diminutive statues of Jesus and Mary, wooden crosses, and a replica of the Ten Commandments. They even had biblical markings written over their car. The only time I witnessed them ever actually leave the home was when they went to church every few days, hastening the week with worship of the Almighty. Any other time, I rarely saw them come outside and socialize.

The family was very soft-spoken, very quiet and often conveyed with whispers, and it seemed as though they purposely avoided interaction with other people. If they needed to access their car in their driveway for any reason, they would walk with their heads bowed, and they would quickly acquire what they needed, ignoring any next-door neighbors that may have been out at the moment. The only time the taciturn family's household became deafening was by nightfall. Torturesome cries and racking yelps and screams could be heard blaring from their daughter's bedroom. Being that the family settled across from my home, I could visually make out where the noise originated, and although the cries came from their daughter in her bedroom, the husband and wife never went into her room to check on her. The light in her room remained off throughout the entire night as she howled like a forsaken dog at the moon. By morning, the family would be back to their usual ways, being socially avoidant and getting through the day by almost tiptoeing around the neighborhood, hoping to appear unnoticed and indiscernible.

Despite the fact that the family stayed secluded into their home the majority of the time, their young daughter would sometimes come outside and play in the front yard throwing rocks, picking the leaves off trees, and poking holes into the dirt with sticks from birch. The child always had a doll with her wherever she went, including church, which she usually kept wrapped in a thin white cloth. The girl didn't seem to have any friends her age, or any friends at all, perhaps being that her parents were both hermits and found no beneficial gratification from interacting with other humans. The girl looked to be very lonely and more so sad, and it became salient by the lugubrious look in her eyes. I would study the girl as she interacted with the doll; she would talk to it, bounce it up and down, cradle and sing to it, and even kiss it on some occasions. She treated the doll as any other five- or six-year-old girl would treat a doll, so I thought no more of it.

I began to feel bad for her and sympathize with her situation because due to her parents, she was unable to make friends. I could see that she would have loved to have other girls her age there with her, exploring her yard, laughing and capering, and playing with her baby doll, but since she could not experience this, she made the best of her dreary predicament. After spending the afternoon with her doll in her yard, her mother or father would open their door and command her to hurry into the house as the day began to grow late; and a few hours later, the same worrisome yelping could be heard from her bedroom.

The vociferation no sooner arose the attention of the residents in the neighborhood, and they began stirring complaints, declaring that the girl's yowling had made it arduous for them to sleep. After reproaching the issue with the girl's father, the neighbors became satisfied with the automatic noiselessness they received. The girl's cries were no longer heard at night, and the neighborhood seemed to retrieve its peacefulness. However, the family did not leave their house for a week after the incident. The girl was no longer seen playing with her doll in her front yard, and the family had even missed church that week. No one in the neighborhood seemed to care as they were only happy that the girl had quit yammering.

I can still recall that one appalling afternoon as if it had just occurred. Police officers virulently escorted the couple out of their home and detained them as other officers heedlessly inspected their house. The wife had asked the officers to let her be as she had just suffered a miscarriage a year ago, and she and her husband were still mourning deeply. Though she had apprised to the officer that she had had a miscarriage, her past hospital records said otherwise. In consideration of her medical history, she had given birth to a male baby a year ago. No male baby had been seen in the couple's home.

To minimize an antic, uncanny story, the woman had given birth to a son over a year ago and had left the hospital the next day after being told that both the child and her were healthy and compatible to leave. While at home, the husband and wife engaged in a potent argument, in which the husband responded out of rage by throwing a large object from the kitchen, which landed on the baby and pulverized his lungs. The hit instantly killed the baby. Not being able to accept what had been done, they continued caring for the baby as if nothing had happened and eventually gave the baby to their oldest child to play with as a doll. The baby was treated as a living person; it was talked to, sung to, rocked, and the girl was even subjected to bathing with the baby. The girl was allowed outside of the house with the baby as long as a cloth is over it so no one would see what it really was and contact authorities.

The baby slept in a bed, in the daughter's room with her. The family even carried the baby to church with them. Although the family had somehow managed to preserve the baby's flesh to keep it from distilling an odor, being that it was still a rotting being that had been uncared for, the family had been open to receiving many life-threatening diseases, the daughter being the contractor. Being around the baby and even going to bed with it, the girl developed Chagas' disease, a disease where Triatominae insects feed on the flesh of a person's face, injecting their blood, and defecating on them. This process only occurred at night, which was why midnight was the only time the family's home became lively. The girl had been suffering from this disease for a few weeks, and the disease had spread and began infecting her organs. The disease also affected her face and her eyelids, stemming from where the insects bit her, and to disguise this, the family concealed her with makeup. It became apparent to me why her eyes always looked guarded with dysphoria.

Since the disease affects major organs, the infection had found its way consuming one of her kidneys. After neighbors had remonstrated with the father about his daughter's wailing, both he and his wife panicked as they believed that if they didn't do anything, they would risk going to jail. So they attempted to remove their daughter's infected kidney, only to fail and witness her take four days to die. After explaining this story to authorities, an officer, filled with complete aghast, recapped the story, making sure that what she had told him had been clearly heard.

"So your husband murdered your child a year ago, and both of you have been caring for the baby and allowing your six-year-old daughter to drag the baby around as a doll before attempting to expel her kidney due to infection?" the officer inquired in an unsettling tone.

"Yes, Officer, but what our daughter has been recently playing with wasn't our baby. That's another child. Our baby depreciated after a few months, so we got her another baby."

Now as a twenty-two-year-old man, this family is the reason why I am now taking courses to become a psychologist.

11

. . . .

Unnaturally, over the years, I evolved into harboring an outlandish fascination for the mentally afflicted, and for some reason, their uncommon methods of thinking had driven me closer to pursuing a career as a competent psychologist. It had to be something about these unsettling, depraved, and maleficent people that attracted me to them, perhaps the fact that a single person could inhabit the attributes to be so inhuman that they could find expunging the life from an impeccable person as permissible.

I wanted to journey into the coarse mind and absorb the little intellect that these degenerates housed and conceive why these people committed the sickening acts that they did. Why and how could someone who asserts that they have an orderly mind-set be so comfortable and complacent with murdering another human being? Normal people do not butcher innocent people. Something has to be profoundly unsound with a "person" who could derive delectation from imposing trauma onto an inculpable individual as they watch them painfully gripe and twinge, knowing that they hold the godlike key to decide whether that person lives or dies. Perhaps that's what murderers relished in, feeling as though they hold some sort of divine endowment over another being by being able to choose who's useless enough to die and who's worthy enough to remain existent. That's what murder is about, control.

What contributed to how these savages perceived the world, what induced them to resort to brutality and intimidation, and if anything, would it be possible to rehabilitate these soulless scoundrels? Is it possible to fix broken glass or, in this case, off-balanced, shattered brains? I believe the unpalatable appeal and interest in these meaningless creatures arose from what I had been exposed to as a child. While persisting through the adversities of my teenage life, my mind haunted me with the same analogous questions. Why did my grandmother murder my grandfather? Why had some careless, sadistic bastard murdered my mother? Why did my overwhelmed father choose the option of committing suicide rather than to face his demons and raise his son as any half-decent doting father would? Why had my grandmother been befouled, violated, and murdered by a fallaciously reliable man who had been unsuspectingly leading people astray by perpetrating malpractice? I did not have these answers at the time, and neither did anyone around me, but I craved the insight that would give me the answer that I longed for dearly.

Though I had forced myself to move past what had happened, an inner utterance always told me that I could never truly be at ease until I located the particular cause behind the actions that had transpired. I felt unfamiliar, curious, and inexperienced, like a toddler inspecting the world around them by gazing at shapes, colors, and bare nature itself.

When I was twenty years of age, my grandfather's health took a turn for the worse when he developed leprosy. His disease caused the doctors to be wrapped in disturbance and tremor because leprosy is an ancient disease, and no one in modern times had been diagnosed with such a ghastly endemic in over a century. The speechless doctors couldn't say anything or do anything but inform my grandfather that he had precisely six months to live. My grandfather never made it to six months. I became my grandfather's legal guardian to guide him through his daily life and monitor whether or not he was receiving his systemic treatment. I had been forced to watch my grandfather's condition advance each day, and after five days, his derma gravely alternated and swelled, morphing into gray, pelt-like matter that began devouring his entire body like a swarm of flies on a deserted carrion. My grandfather's skin appeared similar to a plate filled with crusted, clotted mold, looking like hoary, hardened sand, and having the color of water tainted with black paint. A fog-like, alabaster coloring stained his back, presenting itself as chalky dough and making him look more indisposed than he had already appeared.

Though my grandfather had been the appropriate height for a man, just about six feet and two inches, the disease caused his height to increase; he looked like a melanoid, lengthened pole that laid prostrated across his sepia, senile couch in an "incommodious" form. As my grandfather's skin darkened and began appearing literally black; sapphire streaks consumed the skin on his neck and arms, eventually becoming overcast as well and blending in with his dingy complexion.

The disease cloaked the left side of my grandfather's face and turned it into a blue abyss. The only thing that revealed the left side of his face was his eye, which had decreased in size and stopped functioning. Morsels of his foot began crumbling and falling off, and tiny black holes appeared over his feet and legs, looking like the dainty bites in which ants take out of discarded food.

My grandfather could not physically or vocally express the amount of pang he experienced day after day. Both of his withering feet had already been detached from his legs and left in its place the gray rotted flesh plastered on the thin couch. My grandfather's tan hair fell out, revealing his scalp, which frantically looked like an oil spill. His body continued to reject his limbs as weeks went by, and through all of this, my grandfather spoke no words. He couldn't even eat properly, being in the state of anguish he was in.

On the final day of my grandfather's life, I sat next to what was left of my dear grandfather and reverently comforted him, explaining benevolently that I loved him and that I appreciated how he extended his hand to me when I had nowhere else to go. I told him that he was my grandfather, and I would durably hold him close to my heart as I do my grandmother and my parents. After listening to me speak, his sere face promptly formed a kooky smile, opening and displaying his toothless mouth. An ink-like substance emitted from the crest of his eyes, coloring his pupils black, and in a rapid, jaded voice, he surged, "I am not your grandfather."

With that, his eyes slouched and dangled, drooping from out of his sockets and draping down to the center of the couch, before being fleetly swallowed by the perishing flesh of his depleted chest, leaving him steely and dead. The flesh on his chest seemingly ingested his eyeballs as if his skin had mouths. Immediately, his body became black as tar, leaving the ends of his legs laurel green. His face began to deform itself, revealing an ecru layer that marginally resembled his recognized appearance. The deceased body of my grandfather looked like a burn victim.

That night, without dawdling, I called the hospital for emergency services, reporting that my grandfather had passed after battling two months of leprosy. Being that the location of the nearest hospital settled six hours away, an ambulance was delegated as nimbly as possible. Once I was able to get in contact with any medical attention, I could verify that the paramedics were terrified by what they had seen by the way they viewed and handled my grandfather.

Three days later, after my grandfather had been taken to the morgue, I received a phone call by a concerned mortician. The mortician told me that my grandfather was not human. Crossly, I informed him of my grandfather's condition and that he mustn't be so impudent. The mortician insisted that he was not being disrespectful, but the autopsy results came back, and my grandfather's DNA did not match human DNA. In fact, it matched no distinct DNA. I repeat in the mortician's very words, "I, and no trained professional, know what the hell this is. This is not a person."

Two weeks later, while waiting for the public transportation bus to arrive, I detected my grandfather's minced torso hanging halfway out of the underground sewer. The blood on his shredded torso spelled "Love, Grandpa." Though it was explicitly inescapable, I am the only person who paid any attention.

12

. . . .

No logical exposition granted me the assurance that I could provide for my grandfather the respectable sepulture that he justly earned and deserved because his grinded torso that I had been both unfortunate and fortunate enough to descry wasting away under the sewer had bafflingly vanished. I saw no traces of his dismounted, atrophied flesh tissues in the opaque, begrimed chamber of the atramentous gutter that rested right underneath the manifested bus seat.

The day that I had noticed his hematic disorganized torso loafing out of the sewer gap, I must admit to being emotionally stunned. I had just given my grandfather to a funeral home, and now here he was, dismembered and notched into scattered scraps and left to be seen in broad daylight. I assumed that his body would continue to remain in the same location, seeing as though no one had scrutinized it and had just been sauntering passed it as if nothing were there.

I even paid notice to the few people who had been alert enough to grasp the dead detriment. They gasped with vagary and darted by promptly. I could sense timidity in their eyes. I can recall a small child walking home alone from school and being frightened when a gust of wind captured a large portion of the torso's skin, stripping it off and causing it to clinch to the girl's legs like paper on a blustery fan. The girl shrieked and yanked the slimy skin from around her calves and threw it onto the pavement. Many people saw this take place, but everyone continued to walk straight with their chins in an upraised manner as if they and I were viewing two completely divergent pictures.

The same day, mongrels and children could be seen picking at the skin on the sidewalk and this still stirred no reaction from the absentminded townspeople. I had even witnessed a decomposed dog grip a chunk of the skin in its bleeding mouth and take it home across the street to its owner, and the woman opened the door and let her dog in without caring to observe what her dog had between its teeth.

Afterward, I inspected a mother and her young son walk to find a seat at the bus stop; the child stopped to get a patch of skin from my grandfather's chest. His mother scolded him for picking it up, apprising him that he must honor the dead; she then got down on her knees and placed the cleaved skin back in place of the chest area that her son removed it from. After doing this, she said a succinct prayer, and then she and her child sat down on the bench at the bus stop and acted as if what they just saw and did had been erased from their memories.

Because I had seen such behaviors, I had a strong, unbreakable notion that his remains would sojourn long enough for me to toil on being financially stable in order to afford the necessities for a well-needed funeral. Having a disintegrating human torso plastered in the open streets was shameful, offensive, and repulsive, especially knowing that it belonged to my loved one, but in a condition of being both hapless and nearly beggarly, I had no other choice.

When I discovered that my grandfather's debris had strayed, I became disconcerted, and my mind flooded in nameless wretchedness. I attempted to search for the segregated part, only to receive nothing but failure, which led to me coming in contact with the neglected, hallucinatory horrors of the underground trench. Due to the caliginousness of the sewer, I had complications visualizing much of what I had been scraping over, and though I held a tenacious attitude, a humane volume in my own mind continuously told me to go back, for I could never be prepared to deal with what turpitude awaited my apprehension.

I always ended up leaving in impasse, cursing and disdaining myself for being so inept to being unable find the remnants of my grandfather's frame and give him what I devotedly desired, a funeral to praise him with. I surpassingly resented the situation, being that it caused me to be filled with grief and chagrin, knowing that I could not give tribute and pay my adoration to the man who treated me as a son when my own father abandoned me to die in seclusion. I know my grandfather would have understood my deplorable position, but his understanding did anything but stop me from feeling detestable for not expressing my gratitude for all that he had done for me. If it weren't for my grandmother and grandfather, I would have more than likely committed suicide alongside with my father, assembling myself into nothing more but another improvident spirit who was unable to make way around life's shortcomings and instead took a cowardly way out of the world, only to wind up immured inside of Satan's paradise to be plagued with everlasting iniquities incessantly.

My father believed that by doing what he did, he had escaped hell. Although he may have escaped one level, he had entered an entirely neoteric, unknown hell. And there was no escaping from such a thing. I knew if my father had been in the right frame of mind, he would have gone to the ends of the earth to see that his father had a qualified interment, and because I am the seed of my father, I did just that. I no longer let my own conscience deter me, and after obtaining the courage I required, I bent into the opening of the sewer and groveled and shuffled against unseen excess waste and spilled residue, hoping to uncover what I had been in search of, and abruptly, I did.

As I struggled to identify the cryptic obstacles that guarded my path, I crept onto the ground of the gelid confined sewer, where I eventually came across a dim, effulgent glow that gave me just enough lucent needed for me to examine my surroundings. The closer I managed to crawl and approach the lustrous beam, I believed my exhausted psyche began throwing daunting images into my head as a cautioning for me to retreat, but my stale stubbornness and refusal to be demoted wouldn't accord me the ability to turn away. As I confronted the stomach of the sewer, I found that the light that had been leading me through the conduit had been no more than a small lantern that, instead of a bulb, held ablazing ember. As cold as the inside of the sewer had been, the fire contrarily continued to burn. Beside it, I saw what appeared to be a naked derelict man who had seized the flesh off my grandfather's torso and placed the strips around his shoulders in an attempt to wear it as a jacket. He wrapped my grandfather's vitiated skin around his body and arms, and he seemed to be oblivious to the blood leaking off it. The way the blood dripped and released itself from the skin made it look like a mildewy Italian dish. I could see the skeleton of my grandfather's demolished torso, which he had positioned next to him, splayed and flattened like a rug on a living room floor or a shower curtain in one's bathroom. The skeleton still had some skin plastered on it, and the majority of the ribs had been sundered. As I reached the furthest I would allow my body to attain, I realized that I had been in the presence of a deceased man, and by his appearance, his body had been constrained in the darkness of the sewer for more than a few nights. I stared at his rimy body, not knowing how to react and anticipating for some form of miracle to evacuate me from this repugnant circumstance. His skin had become the color of a glacier. I could see that he had fractured his left foot, causing it to position itself backward and making the bone poke through the ripped skin. Perhaps his injuries had contributed to his death.

I started to query what I should do, if anything at all, and suddenly the entrance to the sewer flung shut, extending the dimness of the sewer and causing it to look like the inside of a cave. Just at that moment, I heard a slight croon coming from the eyes of the man. Listening to the tune, I could ascertain that the humming derived from an aged nursery rhyme. Terrified, I turned the opposite direction and looked for an available trail to guide my way out. Then I heard trivial scuffing. I simulated that it must've been a rodent or some other minuscule creature, and I maintained my task on seeking an exit route. The straggling noise continued, and it sounded like chalk being stabbed on an old blackboard in a quiet room. I looked back and a small opening in the ceiling revealed that the wind had been blowing a folded piece of paper that laid rested in the man's hand. Being nigh enough to observe, I saw that the paper disclosed information to my grandfather's bank account.

13

....

In order to implement myself with an adequate higher education, I unceasingly deliberated on whether or not I should finally act upon marketing my grandparents' home to an accordant person willing to purchase the estate. Settling on the decision to sell my grandparents' home had to be anything but effortless or uncomplicated, respecting the fact that my grandparents slaved and constructed the home into what it had been today. They broke their backs with munificent intentions so they would be able to one day successfully furnish their future grandchildren and relatives with something to look up to and honor, knowing that they'd always have a place to come home to at the end of the day.

Owning a home was something that my grandfather always expressed dignity and pride in; it represented an accomplishment of something that he drudged for and attained alone, also using his achievement as an additional paragon to authenticate that toilsome, strenuous work does eventually remunerate you. I also opened my purposely averted eyes and acknowledged that this home is the same home that my grandparents raised my father into the zealous man that I remember him as in my earlier years, so I felt as though by giving this home away to an arrant stranger, I'd be evincing some form of betrayal to my late generations. I understood the amount of dedication it took one to graduate into owning their own residence, and I just couldn't warrant myself the aptitude to relinquish such a well-deserved acquisition. In my benign mind, I adjusted into believing that selling my grandparent's home would be comparable to tearing down a venerated antique painting or sculpture inconsiderately and destroying it in a brutish and profane manner. How could I degrade my own family? Though the burdens and expectancies of maintaining my grandparents' home financially developed into a hardship that did nothing but cloak me with anxiety and worrisome strains, I held onto the home for as long as my mental health and budgeting would allow me to. I had already gotten accustomed to managing two disparate jobs, and although they gave me a decent amount of money, neither one of them helped me accumulate the financial support needed to keep possession of the home. After receiving erratic monetary abundances, I came to the unfavored conclusion that deciding to commerce my grandparents' house could have been the most reasonable thing that I could have done at the moment.

I began publicly advertising the home through newspaper ads, flyers, and even throughout the internet. Although a populous amount of people earnestly responded to the ads, which resulted in me receiving various phone calls a night, only one person happened to reap my awareness. With my keen discernment and the way he comported, he made himself resemble the befitting purchaser that I had been looking for to turn my grandparents' home over to.

The man went by the name of Grant, and after discussing his past and future intentions of making investments on the home, he mentioned that he used to be a minor musician that performed briefly in the countryside, even going as far as to produce an insufficient amount of records, being that his music never seemed to spark the attention of the majorities. Though he had lived a full life, he begrudged the fact that his short-lived position as a singer and instrument player summarily faded away, leaving him in debt and with nowhere valuable to call a home. He regarded skimming through the daily newspaper and stumbling upon my sale of the home as a form of blessing, seeing that I had made the house affordable and very well suited for an elderly man down on his luck.

Grant's speech pattern made him appear ebullient over the telephone, but coming to adjoin him in person, the man spoke very laconically, the utmost of his words being in his curt greeting. I compulsorily conversed with Grant, divulging further legal aspects of the residence in which I was about to enable him all legal rights to. I informed him that my grandparents' home was now being passed down to him and that although I lamented what I was about to do, it meant nothing considering that it's something that had to be done. Though he didn't speak much, Grant came off as a decorous, deferential man, which is why I could have never imagined him to be involved with or in this case, fortuitously associated with, child bawdiness.

Due to Grant being pecuniary indigent, he allowed a younger man to move into his home as a roommate a month after buying the house. Taking an immediate glance at the man, by his incipient appearance and almost infantile height, he looked to be in his late teens to his early twenties, and he carried himself obnoxiously grungy and disheveled. He always wore stained rickety clothing and precarious boots that crepitated and broke off, responding to his gait. He had an adumbral shade of blonde hair that he seemed to never take the time to sanitize, which in result attached his lengthy, shaggy bangs firmly to his irriguous forehead like leaves on wet concrete.

After discovering that he made a living as a local mechanic one day after watching him arrive home in a work truck with a toolbox securely clutched underneath his left arm, I could partly understand why he always appeared so slovenly, like farm beasts that had been insensibly groveling in streams of sludge and particles of dirt. Since I still resided in the same area, I oftentimes saw this man sitting on his porch with his back turned facing the front door, rambling petty words that made little to no sense to himself, meddling with his fingers and perversely intoning to the tools in his toolbox.

While on my way to work every morning, I sometimes passed by the old house on my way to the bus stop and noticed him facing the opposite direction on the porch. I let my ears wander one day, and I learned that he had given his tools names, some of the names being Dorothy, Lilith, and Darci. After observing this man's behavior and now seeing that he had provided identities to his tools, it became apparent to me that he must have suffered from some sort of mental illness that had been causing him to display these types of concerning behaviors, including the disregard for his own personal hygiene. I wanted to commute with him in an effort to show him that I was in his favor, my way of displaying my understanding of him.

One afternoon I discerned him as he happened to be arriving home from work. I introduced myself to the man in a welcoming manner and asked for his name in return. He looked at me as if I had said something foreign, like an animal would look at a human being or like children being introduced for the first time on a playground, and he churlishly mumbled to himself and proceeded to unlock his front door. He instantaneously locked the door after shutting it, and he lowered the blinds to his living room. I assumed that his inability to communicate derived from the disorder clogging his mental processes, and I concluded that being courteous and respecting that would have been the finest understanding I could have exhibited.

I can remember one morning as I watched Grant rake the leave in his yard while his roommate sat on the porch doing the exact same thing with his tools. He would address his tools by the same names in a tender, polite voice, sounding like a mother talking to her newborn baby. I asked Grant to speak with me in private, and after abiding to my request, I asked him if he had taken note to any of the things that his roommate had been doing. Grant told me that he was on the verge to asking him to leave, sensing that his life was in peril, being that he constantly felt skittish around him. Grant told me that his roommate would sit alone in his room, with the door locked and his blinds sealed, having detailed conversations with his tools, groaning and strangely informing them that they mustn't tell their parents. The names Lilith and Dorothy ordinarily came up more than the other names did, showing that he held affinity to those contrivances.

Grant told me that his roommate did this every single night without fail, and that he was too aghast to confront him about it. Grant said his roommate never came out of his room to eat either; the only time he left the bedroom was when his boss called him in for work. Grant said that after his roommate received a call from his boss telling him to come into work for a late shift, he patiently waited until he got into his truck and left, and then he went into his room and dialed the number that his roommate had just recently got done speaking to. Perplexingly, the number was not even real. Grant went through his list of contacts and newly dialed numbers and found that none of them were existent numbers. Most of the numbers that had been dialed were nothing more but 666.

He described his room as chaotic and clustered, being flooded with inutile papers, pornographic magazines, and pamphlets that issued information about the well-being of children.He had two desktop computers,both that had been unplugged; one of them had lacked a keyboard and other purposive parts, and although both computers were in no condition to be used, his roommate spoke about browsing online throughout the day. After being withdrawn for most of the night, his roommate would come back in at around one to two in the morning and go straight to his room. After some brief minutes of silence, he could hear him talking to his tools again and complimenting "Dorothy."

Grant told me that this had been going on for the past week, and it's been disturbing him more and more as the days progressed. To me it proved to be unbelievable that the once silentious and reserved man that I had sold my grandparents' home to was now opening up and being garrulous about appalling matters. I enlightened Grant on how his roommate had responded to me the other afternoon when I introduced myself and asked him for his name. I then asked Grant what his name was. Grant told me that his roommate told him that he didn't have a name, even going as far as to say that his corpse had been buried years ago. Listening to this irrational information, I assured Grant that he would be fine as long as he stayed out of his way and waited until the end of the month to serve him an eviction notice.

My only regret was that I did not take Grant fully pensive about all that he had been telling me, and maybe if I would have paid mind to these seemingly fictitious tales, he would still be alive and breathing today. I received information while watching the news broadcast a couple of days later that Grant had been murdered in his home by four men, all of them being fathers and somehow correlated to one another. While his roommate was supposedly working a night shift, the four men had forced an entry into Grant's home, bounding and restraining the decrepit man using ineluctable twine.

Then they proceeded to slice both his ears off with a boning knife, preluding by trimming off the tips of his ears with a miniature blade and severing the edges gradually as they gorged a brick of wood inside of Grant's mouth, in an attempt to prevent him from shrilling. As Grant contended to extricate himself from the excruciating restraint that the flagitious man had held him confined in, the brick of wood that had been compacted into his mouth began to crack, shattering in his mouth and cutting the insides of both his cheeks. It stabbed unobtrusive holes into the inside walls of his mouth and caused his cheeks to bleed. The scrambled pieces of wood deluged down his throat, denuding the meat of the inside of his neck and forming crevices into his windpipes.

After disjoining both of Grant's ears, the men placed his severed ears into the now open holes on the side of his head before searching his home and acquiring his idiophones. The trespassers held Grant's idiophones and clashed them beside the open gaps of his head, increasing his pain by ejecting an intolerable tremor that punctured the now swollen pockets, making the caverns on the sides of his head stretch wider and more loosely; allowing them to look similar to holes on an overgrown garbage disposal.

As Grant lay there on his bedroom floor exuding blood from the sectors of his head while his throat indolently leaked from its several assorted cuts, two of the men exited the room while the other two continued to build onto Grant's anguish, flicking the split skin from around the areas that they disunited his ears from and spreading it in different directions, causing it to break and pull off into their hands.

The other two men who had been absent returned to his bedroom, both of them holding equipment to Grant's voluminous amplifier. Grant began to totter and turbulently quiver on his sides as if he had been caught in an earthquake, and the two men clasped him down by his chest and stomach, tightening the thread that restricted him from moving, causing him to attempt to catch his breath and release a vocal vibration as the other men assembled his amplifier. The men exposed an undersized dusty black tape; they inserted it into Grant's VCR and connected it to his amplifier. After organizing the device into use, the men obtrude the wires to the amplifier into the exposed hollows of Grant's head, placing them deep into the holes and pull- ing them together so that both wires meet inwardly into the center of his head. They operate the machine, enabling a slightly weak sound to flow through the passageway of his head, which sounds like the ethereal ringing that people endure during auditory tests.

Grant began to cringe with discomfort and thrust his head side to side, and after seeing this, the men gradually increased the volume. The ringing sooner evolved into high-pitched, overly despondent bewailing; it sounded like the watered-down cries of toddlers and infants, and after just seconds, the noise becomes rambunctious and diabolic. The ghastly tone slid from the amplifiers like a serpentine and possessed the entire house with its sinister sound, Grant holding the weight of the stricken recipient, being that he has both wires engraved into his head. As the sound grew, Grant struggled to speak out, but it was difficult for him to do so because the wood that had chipped in his mouth earlier had slashed the veins in his tongue.

A person's voice can be heard from the audio, and based on the tone and the use of language, one can conclude that the voice belonged to a little girl. The voice said, "Why are you doing this to us?" Comprehending the words coming from the voice was abstruse because the dialect kept fading in and out, like wind near an open window. The intonation began affecting Grant's body, and blood poured from his nose like the water from a watering can. Both his eyes began to bleed, dilating and spreading apart, and swiftly bursting alongside with his nose and certain sections on the right side of his head, causing him to die.

The impact caused his nose to diminish and propel, leaving behind nothing but cruor seeping from his inorganic, disfigured face. The four men who murdered him were apprehended five days later and taken into custody. Grant had been affiliated with something that he had known nothing about. The men who murdered him had been looking to exact retribution on his roommate for what he had been doing, and after finding out where he stayed, they acted out their infuriation with the first person that they saw at home. They assumed Grant to have been involved with the acts as well, and that he had known what had been transpiring, allowing him to harbor his roommate to keep him secure.

Unfortunately, neither one of these scenarios were the case. Grant had been ignorant of his roommate's enigmatic lifestyle and had purposely desisted himself from him in fear of his life. He had no knowledge of what his roommate had been doing while alleging that he had been working the night shift at an auto shop. Prior to renting a room inside of Grant's home, his roommate had abducted three small girls at his local park, all of them being Caucasian, brunette, and close to the same age. Apparently, he had been observing them for quite a while, and he decided to finally act upon his fantasies and mold them into his reality. After applying a liquefied stimulant to an undetectable handkerchief in hopes of inflicting drowsiness, he transported the unconscious girls to a desolate hotel room, where he had been holding them hostage for weeks, raping them and videotaping the acts and selling the videos to provincial sex shops and residents willing to buy them. He had even been charging men around the area to come to the hotel room and watch him as he polluted the young girls with both his reproductive organs and various weapons and appara- tus. He had taken pictures of the majority of the practices that he had imposed on the girls, nearly half of them being stored under his bed and crumbled beneath all the trash that guarded his bedroom.

Taking one glimpse at any of the pictures presented would make any sane person regurgitate. One of the photos depicted a small child positioned downward with her chest planted onto the ground in a galling formation, possibly deafening while an unknown person shoved an unwieldy handspike deep into her rectum, dividing the structure of her buttocks and tearing her rectum completely ajar, similar to ringent lips. The picture had been snapped from the inside of a closet full of mites and cockroaches, many of which were teeming over the child's unclad body. A later picture obtained exposed another small girl who had been forced to give several unidentified men fellatio while a man disguised in a mask dissected her genitalia with a hardened trench. Both of these girls were covered in massive amounts of feces, which shielded their eyes, mouths, and their limbs from being recognized, and the third girl was shown covered in both feces and the semen from scads of men. She had been violated to the point that she had gone permanently blind and could no longer breathe properly from her nostrils.

A snapshot revealed that the men had succeeded in merging the girl's tongue to the roof of her mouth and cementing her lips entirely shut with their bodily fluids. Due to the binding of her mouth, the girl suffered days without eating and stayed sheltered away in the closet bleating like a calf and desperately attempting to unglue her mouth from the arrangement that the men fastened it in, only to fail and end up ripping the roof of her mouth off and choking to death on her own blood.

Most of the videos that the roommate had sold to people captured him and other physically veiled men defecating on the girls, feeding them the excrement, and shoving their semen down their throats with a screwdriver. Acts such as these had been perpetuating for weeks before all three of the girls died from exhaustion, being able to no longer bear it anymore.

The killers of Grant had been researching information about the identities of all the men shown in the videos and pictures, and belatedly, they gained access to the address of one of them. The four men then came forth and disclosed that they were the fathers of the three girls exploited in the pictures and tapes, and one of the men was an uncle of one of the girls. They confessed to the murder of Grant, going into detail about how they killed him, informing the detectives in the interrogation room that they had went into a room in the man's house and came across the material needed to know that this man must have been a participant, perhaps one concealed in a mask.

The tape that they used to torture Grant with was the audio of their daughters being raped and impaled. When the thorough truth arrived and the men learned that they had murdered an innocent man, they could do nothing but sit in silence and be wrapped with bottomless sorrow and self-hostility. They had neglected to procure justice for their daughters and niece, Dorothy, Lilith, and Darci. It didn't even take a month for the men to receive a conviction. The courts sentenced all four to life in prison.

It now became evident to me as to why Grant's roommate labeled his tools by human female names; they were in reference to the girls he had been holding captive. Pondering about it, he had possibly been using those same tools he carried around to maim them. It also dawned on me as to why he had been dialing 666 repetitively on his phone. He had kidnapped three girls, and all of them happened to be aged six. He became infected with an obsession for these girls, dedicating every moment of his life to these children and centering around them like chairs near a table. In his mind, he thought that by the things he did, he was portraying love.

A week after the men's sentencing, authorities located Grant's late roommate strapped onto train tracks with laden twine. Sighting the officers, he beseeched they intervene and help release him from the tracks, whimpering and mewling for them to conserve his life. The officers overlooked his pleas and watched as a train speedily drove into his genitals. His last words being, "Why are you doing this to me?"

14

....

D amnable emotions of despondency abducted my mind and altered the way that I beheld a somewhat "hopeful" and promising perception of the world that I persisted in and made me utterly conscious of the inexcusable culpabilities and iniquitous actions of society and humanity as a whole the minute I observed what had been done to the whilom home of my expired grandparents.

After the murder of Grant, an uproar and protest for rectitude arose from the town once most of its people had learned about the three girls that had been seized and raped by a passel of incognito men, and no sooner after that, my grandparents' residence had been rearranged into an exiguous center that offered aiding services by counselors and help with becoming financially stable to victims of rape and other intolerable, obscene sex crimes.

The intention behind the center seemed to be essentially helpful and convenient for women and young girls who had been compelled to surrender to such hideous, baneful enormities and go about in life with the psychological misery and the grueling wounds that had been left carved into their minds from having to experience such things from absolute demonic, perverted, and mentally warped savages and dissolute beasts of the earth.

To be entirely veracious, after being informed about the town's plan for my "grandparents" home, it gave me faith and confidence in the world; perhaps our civilization didn't view righting a wrong as an impossibility, especially if the foundation of the right existed to be in favor of the less powerful and for the people who did not have a voice, such as the small, inferior children who had tolerated such contemptible torment without anyone even holding the awareness to know where they were located. I supported the outcome and embraced the reality that although that home used to belong to my grandparents, they were no longer alive to cherish it; and due to my financial shortcomings, it had practically shifted into an abandoned property. Because of this, I thought of it as being only impartial that their home be donated to a productive cause, something that they themselves would have promoted being the sympathetic, kind-spirited people that they lived as. I accepted the current decision as a form of a resolution, something that would finally bring mindfulness and alert people about the misuse and cruelty toward women and young female children.

While awaiting for such a change to come forth, leaving the barbaric practices behind and anticipating for a progressive chapter to arrive, my vision exposed itself to be no more than just that. Just a simple, seemingly prudent vision. Due to the fact that I had already gripped the appeasing idea of useful resources catering to defenseless women in desideratum of guidance, a person to listen to them, and perhaps even a shoulder to lean on, my parlous, elated attitude displaced itself with a darkly, stupefied demeanor once I saw what despicably hellish, morbid, and almost fictional burlesque this asserted efficacious establishment had morphed into. If only the sickening actuality could have been fortunate enough to be no more than fiction. With the first gander that I happened to make at this freakish, substantive horror parade, I automatically polished both my eyes with the ends of my shirt to confirm that this was truly something that my eyes were grasping and that my mind hadn't been satanically deforming my psychological conception in some noisome, perverse attempt to be facetious, because at that very moment, portending apparitions inhabited my soul as if I had been ignorantly lingering on a haunted terrain. I espied what arose to be some sort of a puppet-like figurine that the care center had firmly patched into the soil with a gangling slat of wood that they had implanted on the backside, with the possibility of using the figure as an adornment or as an inviting way to attract those with the yearning for their services, exacting to further validate that they're solicitous.

From afar, the figure looked to be anything but welcoming, more so nightmarish, concluding that the center had, for some odd unexplained reason, installed a solemn, fuscous debased puppet in the yard of their business, seeming to discard the fact that the ornament looked bleakly tarnished and dauntingly mutilated. Its opaque, misshapen, and featureless head crouched to the left as if the inanimate being had a mangled neck, reminding me of the incommo- dious position that artisans usually station Christ in most of their compositions. Due to the figure being dishabille, I could detect fulsome openings that the figure had in the front of its body, as if it were the victim of numerous stab- bings. All of them looked like the slanted holes in brutally torn jeans. Inside of the extensive slits draped abnormally large clumps of bole-colored cotton that dangled like a necklace and carelessly wandered in the graceless gust. The figure's arms hung nearly disjointed, swaying in a tilted manner like a tree's branches after suffering through a vehement squall, and tense strings wielded down its arms in a docile arrangement, which led me to wonder if the fig- ure had perhaps just been a repulsive marionette. Both of the puppet's feet were imperceptible and looked similar to intensely burnt obsidian, and they appeared to have indurate, mauve veins streaming down the centers, connecting themselves to the figure's stumped appendages.

Why would a supposed "caring" and "nurturing" clinic allow such a macabre object to represent a significant subject matter? Could this startling display have possibly just been a cruel, depraved joke? What if the idea of this small organization had not been something meant to presume seriously?

While continuing to look at this grotesque mockery and scope out more of its teratoid malconformation, I saw an undersized assembly of people gathering around together in a taut circle. They were examining the stiff figure and seemingly discussing its quality and appearance as if they were art critics judging a workmanship by its design, texture, and dexterity. The small crowd of people joined hands and bowed their hands as if they were praying, and after ostensibly adjuring, the people formed together like a flock of fowls and lifted up a pasty, cherub-like child. They hoisted her to the top of the figure and allowed the child to rub the face of the dummy and get an applicable grip of it. The child stably clamped the face of the figure like a hair clip, peculiarly causing her fingers to facilely enter the figure's face as if it had been water.

As the people prepared to lift her down, it confounded me to see that their dispositions had sorely altered, and infuriation could be sensed by the venomous cast bawling from out of their now shadowed, vermillion-clouded eyeballs. Their eyes radiated like the color of a street light signaling for drivers to hindrance in the heart of a vaporous midnight. One of the adults eradicated a wooden belt from around his waist in an attempt to scold the child for whatever she had done wrong. The belt consisted of scabrous, barbed, erected layers lodging from out of each of its edges, looking similar to a merciless torture weapon used in a medieval era. The child showed signs of aghast and panic as she attempted to shelter her face and her upper body the most she could with her nuga- tory hands.

The imprudent man yanked the threatening strap from around his distended waist frantically and expeditiously clutched the girl's face with the arboraceous hook of the belt, digging into the child's face like a carabiner would do on a boulder. It captured small pieces of her skin, carving it off like a grater, slickly peeling off her entire face like a sticker and making the girl's face hang wedged onto the serrated ends of his belt, oscillating off the piercing thorns in a sloppy manner.

Unnervingly, after exfoliating the young girl's face, the man withdrew her now dead, detached face from his belt, and I watched as he spread apart the dirt from underneath his feet with both his hands; unconcernedly exposing the defunctive faces of various other children who had by now all shrunken and parched like raisins and decolorized into unilluminated slabs of abjected, rotted amethyst. He lightly planted the girl's face down into the middle of the divided walls of the dirt next to another child's face, and he positioned it upwardly so that it blended in with the rest. The man then kneeled down and osculates the face's lips passionately. In order to complete his eccentric motive, he crawled over to the girl's lifeless body and begins lasciviously sucking her tongue, absorbing its dead fluids and draining the remaining color that had been left of it, leaving it a sallow, Cambridge blue. The tongue is the only half functioning organ left on the girl's face, next to her nostrils and her drifted eyes; she didn't have a nose because it was attached to her face when the man pulled it off. I could tell that her tongue had still been able to operate as it looked to be fluttering lazily like a desiccated fish on a torrid surface.

Just as the man began to swallow the tarrying sap from the child's moribund tongue, a frothy drizzle came into existence, causing the dirt in which the people had been standing on to liquefy, moistening the soil and making it propel downward, eventually veering and bringing to light a replete row of gleaned, spectral-like decomposed faces.

I couldn't fully accept and take into mind what had been in front of me. An entire garden suffused with the heisted flesh of children's visages. Some of the faces had achingly fiendish smiles. Others didn't have smiles because their faces didn't even contain lips. I could see infinitesimal pairs of hoary lips buried into the dirt next to the faces, assuming that they had belonged to the children that they were stripped off of. What the hell was this abhorrence, and what happened to the bodies of these children? Witnessing such reprehensible deeds take place gave me an unbearable migraine and made me feel nauseated, and as I contended through a pulsating headache, that was when most of my questions presented themselves with the unearthly answers.

After the man finished draining the residuum from the dead tongue, he picked up the girl's body and raised it to the face of the figurine. After doing so, he and the other people displayed satisfaction and gaiety by expelling their leer and the ferocious glow in their eyes. Surprisingly, they looked just as they did before they had decided to allow the girl to brush against the figure, like ordinary, common people, if not, more blissful. They convened closer and began applauding themselves while looking up to the faint puppet, proceeding to reach into the puppet's stomach area and rashly tear out its cotton and sprinkling it atop of the girl's body and burying her with it. Evidently, this girl had not been the only child who had undergone this procedure, paying mind to the untoward cemetery of the other godforsaken children.

What I thought would be a community service devoted to improving the lives of female rape victims and survivors of child molestation had turned into something only a truly licentious bastard could imagine. Instead of contributive counselors and therapists managing the organization, it had been consumed by former bloodcurdling pedophiles who had convinced themselves that it was the child to blame for being a victim of rape or molestation, stating that if the child weren't attractive, they wouldn't have been targeted; and since the majority of children are attractive, they outright deserve anything unsound that happens to them.

The owners of the center had been attempting to defect the face of children, believing that by taking away a child's face, they would be taking away the child's attractiveness, therefore calming the urges of many men like them. As the details of the infamous account proceeded, the almost unbelievable tale began to become increasingly maleficent as I shoveled deeper into the center of the disturbing occurrence.

These diseased pedophiles had located the pestiferous carcass of Grant's roommate tied rigidly onto the reclusive train tracks while on their way to lay to rest a dead child, and they discovered that his body had been entirely concealed and disguised by an inordinate pile of hookworms, flesh-devouring isopods, and parasites so small that they could not be detected by the naked eye. The innumerable amount of insects had been sluggishly dragging across his body in odious clusters, taking mere bites out of his vert dead skin and hatching more insects on top of the others. Because there had been mountains of vermin scattered across his body, the men found it difficult to tell apart which arachnids were alive or dead, only being able to notice that the majority of the insects had begun consuming one another, even devouring their newly born offspring and the formerly dead motes. What a grody sight to perceive, the insects bustled over the deceased in the pattern of a crossword puzzle.

Once the men laid down the girl's body next to the corpse, the parasites promptly bolted onto her body and began gorging it, leaving the dead and half-eaten louses behind, plastered on the other body. Although the insects had chewed the corpse's face away, the men could distinguish who the person had been by its torn plaid shirt and some remaining identifiable traits on its face. Its faded azure-colored jeans had been shredded in the front, revealing that it had been a male body by its rived testicles and a dehisced void indicating that it used to have a penis. Recognizing that the body belonged to Grant's roommate, the person whom they had been buying child pornography from, the men cleared some of the rapacious pests off of it, and one of them untied the body and transported it back with them into the city and positioned it like a scarecrow in the front yard of the care center.

These men then acquired rights to the center and had been using it since to attract other pedophiles and bring young children to present them to the cadaver placed near the establishment. The purpose behind raising the child to the face of the mortified bairn rapist arose from the belief that children bring rape upon themselves by their innocence. When they lifted the child to the body, if the body resonated, that was a signal that the body found the child attractive. So the children would no longer be alluring, the men pulled off the child's face, placed it into the ground, and then finished by lifting the child back up to the body. When the men heard nothing more, they took the child's body down to the train tracks where they nourished the parasites. Many people in the area became accustomed to this persuasive practice, and they began bringing their children to these deranged people. They had been defacing and killing multiple children each day as a way to mask their sickness and control the temptation. I couldn't react after I had seen such a thing. I had watched these people pull out the insides of a carcass and pile it on top of a faceless withering child.

These people had grown to the idea that a body had been communicating with them by generating noises, but they had been unaware of the fact that the body hadn't been making a single sound. The only thing that they had been hearing were the sounds of tools clinking together in the body's back pocket. The sounds could have also possibly derived from the abounding amount of lymantrid moths and Stenopelmatus that had dug tunnels inside of the corpse's face, tightly packing into its already decomposed jowls like money in a wallet and falling into the piceous abyss of its absent lower jaw.

Once law enforcement received knowledge about these heinous, unutterable abominations, the men who had committed the vile crimes were sentenced to death by the flaying of their groins. Eventually the scandalous care center was terminated. Authorities acknowledged the town's residents' concurrence on the illegal verdict, and after doing so, the residents participated in the dreadful yet just retribution, interning the men to an afflictive panel of wood, similar to that of which they had had Grant's roommate's corpse constrained to. The residents proceeded by using a knout to briskly obtain and tear off the flesh on their penises, striking and snatching off its outer layer repeatedly until their skinless inflamed puce genitals produced unsightly blisters and open wounds, causing the split lacerations to trickle jots of blood. Because of the impetuous thrashing that the now frantic men had writhed through, the horrid ending results of the impairment left their obliterated genitals with the resemblance of haggard, shrunken earthworms.

After pillaging all the tissue from the men's sexual organs, the residents gathered the scraps of skin, which had by then diffused across the begrimed ground due to the forceful yanking, and the residents buried the skin into the dirt, positioning it upward so that all of it blended in together.

To twinge the men to a surpassing extent, the residents began absorbing the sodden blood from their ravaged shafts, causing the traumatized men to screech in unendurable agony, before abandoning them to perish in the deary, postmeridian atmosphere.

A couple of days later, prior to the grisly bloodstained calamity, I peered a man who had been sitting in an open field using the rotted hand of the leech-infested corpse of Grant's roommate to vaginally penetrate a five year old girl. The man seemed to mistake the girl's uproarious shrills for sounds of satisfaction, and he wielded the putrid limb to carve deeper into the shredded void, eventually paring her organ completely off with the sordid nails of the corpse. The small girl shrieked and wailed vociferously, and the man began to suck the sinuous blood from out of the maimed gap while continuing to use the corpse's hand to finger her disconnected genitalia.

The man looked familiar as if I had just seen him recently, and it then arose to me as to why I had recognized his anterior. This man had been one of the officers who had helped sentence the pedophiles to their brutal penalty, and now here he was, molesting a little girl with a corpse.

I knew that I had to disenthrall myself from this aberrant town and its villainous residents in strong fret of eventually mutating into one of them myself, and with invulnerable willpower, I complied with my innate self-morality. Now in the city of El Paso, I began taking psychology seminars at my nearest community college where I came in contact with my amoral, salacious, German psychology professor, Charles Fiktion, and unfavorably stumbled upon the most baneful cancer to the human species itself. Lanza Bhoardar-Lionel.

SkylerrDarren

CPSIA information can be obtained
at www.ICGtesting.com
Printed in the USA
LVHW081943120219
607106LV00020B/19/P

9 780692 872253